THE BIG PICTURE

Andrew J. Simpson

BareBackPress

This is a work of fiction. The characters, incidents, and dialogue are the products of the author's imagination and are not to be construed as real. Any resemblance to actual events or person, living or dead, is entirely coincidental.

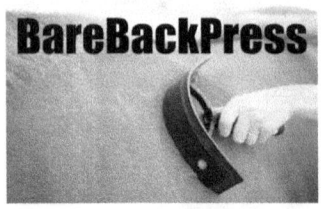

BareBackPress
Hamilton, Ontario, Canada
For enquires visit www.barebackpress.com
For information contact press@barebacklit.com
Cover layout by Choi Yunnam

CONTENTS

Jones 9

Myers Motors Can't Be Beat 11

Happily Ever After 15

Madagascar 20

Graham Ericsson Dies 22

Marla 26

Sapiens Versus Neanderthalensis 31

Kissing 34

Historical Accuracy 38

The Wrong Side of the Bed 41

The Meek 46

Broadway 49

Creative 53

Forgetting the Alamo 56

Hagen 59

The David 65

2014 68

Catsup 72

The Nice List 76

The Lonely 78

A Melpaso Production 81

Love 88

Time's Person of the Year 90

Jaczek 93

The Dream Tax 100

2.1 103

Thirtysomething 108

I Love You 115

Adrian 118

Assertiveness Training 121

The Monster Under the Bed 123

Lost and Found Love 128

Childhood Memories 132

Baseball 134

Winners 136

Geography Class 139

The Compass 142

The Tits of a High School Girl 149

Real 153

It Couldn't Have Happened to a Nicer Guy 155

The Big Picture 158

All You Need is Love 162

BMX 166

Photographic Evidence 169

Like In Roshomon 172

IQ 176

Ordinary 179

The Moment 182

Bernie 187

The Girl Next Door 189

Right in the Middle of Something 191

Murphy 196

My Reputation 199

Good Riddance Matthew Goldman 206

My Neighbour's Dog 210

The Average Price of a Cup of Coffee in Seattle 215

The Success Audit 218

Soul Mate 222

How it Ended 228

Repeat 230

Jones

There are no original ideas left. None. Everyone knew it was dire, but they didn't know how bad it was until they posted the list of ideas that hadn't been had and it was empty. Theologians from all religions and spiritualists and agnostics and even atheists have been filing access to information requests with the cosmos for over a decade to try to get hold of the list. With the last idea gone, there was no more reason to hold up its publication.

From now on, every idea everyone has has been had before. There was one original idea still out there and it was that fucker Jones that got it. It's not a very good idea. You don't even really understand it. It's something to do with hedgehogs.

That's not the point, though. The point is Jones, who's kind of an idiot, had the last original idea in the universe and now you're stuck with nothing. You can still prove or disprove existing ideas, or put together two ideas that have never been put together before, but there's nothing that's truly new.

Everything's been thought of and you got nothing. You had forty years to come up with something, even something stupid involving hedgehogs, but no. Jones, who dropped out of university and drives a truck for Fed-Ex and whose wife left him because he was such a bum, he's better than you. And the worst thing is Jones never even tried to be original. It just happened. One day an idea came into his otherwise empty head. That's more than ever happened in your head.

It's depressing and you want to cry, or bash Jones' head in and steal his idea. You're the first person he's told his idea to. There are problems with bashing in his head, though. For one thing, you don't entirely understand his idea, so it doesn't do much good to steal it. And for another, somebody thought up things like murder charges and jail and even if you had a good plan for getting rid of Jones, somebody's thought of the plan before, and somebody might think of the plan again and realize that's how you did it.

Besides, you don't have a plan right now and by the time you come up with one that moron Jones will have called his mom and told her about his idea.

So you're fucked. You'll have to live with the fact that there are no more ideas out there and that Jones had the last original idea, and no matter how long you live, you'll never have an idea of your own.

Myers Motors Can't Be Beat

I died. I never really believed in an afterlife, but there is one. I showed up after I died and I was in a room with painted brick walls. It stank like mildew. A bunch of guys sat on wooden benches that went around the walls and chanted, "Myers Motors can't be beat."

"Hey, he's with us," somebody said and they sat me down in the corner.

Myers Motors was the first hockey team I played with. When I was eleven. Our cheer was, "1, 2, 3, 4, 5, 6, 7 all great hockey players go to heaven. When they get there, they repeat, Myers Motors can't be beat."

It was what every team in the league cheered, just with their name instead of ours. Their name was whoever'd paid to sponsor the team, same as ours.

"So this is heaven?" I said.

"Damn straight," John said.

"There's even a league up here," Dan said.

"Oh yeah? How are we doing?" I said.

"We're one and seventeen. We kicked the shit out of this Mexican novice team that went down in a plane crash," Mike said.

"So we can be beat," I said.

"It all comes down to championship time. We can't be beat when it counts."

"We didn't even win our league. We came second."

It was vicious in heaven. Teams screamed back and forth at each other insisting that they couldn't be beat. The Montreal Canadiens and the Philadelphia Flyers both beat us by more than a hundred goals.

It was that kind of crazy competition everywhere. Each morning the crusaders rode out onto the battlefield against the jihadists and the winners took on the winners of the Romans versus the Parthians. Everybody'd moved to modern technology. You could hear the explosions and gunfire from miles away.

At the hockey complex, Myers Motors went 0 and 26 with me on the team. After losing twenty-six in a row, I quit. I walked out of the dressing room after the first period of a game and went home.

Some guys accosted me on the way. "Hey, you can't just quit. Myers Motors can't be beat. Now you've got to prove it," one of them said.

"Look. I wasn't a great hockey player," I said. They looked at me and at each other, confused. "I wasn't even a good hockey player. This is bullshit."

They sighed. "Fine." They threw me in the back of a van and took me in to this office. I had to stand in front of a woman behind a desk that came up to my chest and explain to her how I didn't want to play for Myers Motors anymore.

"I see," she said. "You played on several hockey teams. You played the longest for your high school team. Would you like us to put you with them?"

"No."

"Well, we don't allow people here to just sit around and do nothing," she said.

She looked through a file for a bit. Then she went into a back room and made a phone call. She came out with a yellow t-shirt with green trim and handed it to me.

"Put this on please. These men will escort you," she said.

The men put me in a wandering troupe of people all dressed in the same t-shirts. I recognized some of them. We made our way around heaven, from the battlefields to the hockey rinks to the ball diamonds to the soccer pitches and to the gymnasiums. Everywhere we went people stopped what they were doing and asked us who we were.

We told them we were from Severn, Mighty, Mighty Severn and then we had to explain that it was an elementary school in the west end of Ottawa, Canada and not a river in Britain.

It wasn't much fun, but it beat the hell out of losing by a hundred. Or it did until we met up with a wandering troupe from the Severn region in Britain. Severn was a K to 6 school and we were like ninety students when I was there.

The English group challenged us to a fight and they kicked our asses. After that we kept wandering. People still asked who we were and we still told them "We're from Severn, Mighty, Mighty Severn."

A couple of days after getting beat up by the group from the Severn River, we ran across Charlemagne and some soldiers. We told them we were from Severn, Mighty, Mighty Severn and they took it as a challenge. It didn't go well for us.

After that, I quit the troupe. Some guys came out again and hauled me back to the office where I had to stand in front of the woman with the high desk.

"Stop being difficult," she said.

"Look, when I was a kid, I don't remember anyone asking who we were. Ever. This whole thing is just stupid," I said.

"We could set you up with another former institution. Would you like to bleed blue and grey perhaps?"

"No."

"Well, I'm afraid then that we are running out of options."

"I played baseball when I was a kid, right?" I said.

I was never much good at baseball, but Joe's Car Radio is four and two since I started playing for them. Unfortunately, we play the Yankees four in a row starting Monday and there's no mercy rule in heaven, so it could take weeks.

Happily Ever After

Disney held a Happily Ever After Lottery™. It was the first worldwide lottery. Tickets were available in every country in the world and there was no limit on the number of tickets you could buy.

The tickets cost five dollars American, no matter where you were. Somebody asked why it wasn't on an ability to pay basis.

"The less you have, the more you need this, the more, relatively speaking, you're willing to pay," a spokesman for Disney said.

Disney made a mint off the lottery. People all over bought tickets like mad. The rich divested portfolios and the middle-class took out second mortgages. In developing countries employers offered tickets in lieu of pay.

Madeleine spent six thousand on tickets. That was her savings, mine and the money on the joint credit card. Madeleine won, which didn't make anyone else happy. The Americans were pissed that an American corporation would let a Canadian win the inaugural lottery, and the international community was pissed that people in underdeveloped countries spent everything they had and yet the odds of someone outside the first world winning were approximately one in a trillion.

Those thoughts weren't important for Madeleine because she won. That meant happiness, and thoughts about other people's suffering were annoying.

When Madeleine won, I was excited, but then Disney came and got her and left me.

"Hey, what gives?" I said.

"She lives happily ever after, not you," they said.

"Yeah, but her happily ever after must include me somehow."

"Sorry," they said.

"Sorry," Madeleine said.

"Almost half that money was mine. How do you know which five bucks the winning ticket was bought with?" I said and they got me out of the apartment.

I went back that night and almost everything was left behind. Even most of Madeleine's clothes. She took the dog and the teddy bear she'd had since she was three and a half.

I packed up my stuff and moved to a smaller place. By myself I couldn't afford the rent where we'd been living. I left all of Madeleine's stuff, except for a t-shirt and a pair of underwear, and the landlord charged me three hundred bucks to get rid of it.

Shit was tough all over Canada. People had spent everything to try and win the Happily Ever After Lottery™. Houses were being abandoned by people who couldn't make their mortgage payments, and seniors were getting tossed out of retirement homes.

The governments knew they had to step in, but they were broke because a year's worth of lottery money had gone to Disney instead of to them. It was the same in the US and Europe too. People agitated for a general cancellation of debts like they used to do in ancient Rome.

In the developing world people had borrowed against several years' worth of salary to buy their tickets and they were suddenly working for nothing.

Disney wasn't bothered by any of this, because they were swimming in money. They started planning a second Happily Ever After Lottery™, but countries refused to license it. It took three years for Disney to hammer out a deal with the world's governments. The governments tried to play hardball with Disney, but they couldn't afford to. In the end they settled for a lump sum payment and Disney had their lottery.

The lump sum payment wasn't nearly enough. People spent even more on the second lottery than they had on the first and the governments were squeezed even more tightly.

I thought a lot about Madeleine still. At night I cuddled with her t-shirt and her underwear. I'd always been obsessed with Madeleine. When I'd asked her out and she'd said yes, I couldn't believe it. Neither could my friends. Then she won the lottery and she left me.

When the second lottery came around, I spent everything I had. With a line of credit I managed to buy eleven thousand dollars worth of tickets.

I didn't win. The winner was a twenty-eight year old from Manhattan named Matt. Matt was an investment banker. He spent over a billion dollars of his clients' money on tickets, but it didn't matter that he'd misappropriated his clients' money because he'd won, so he got to be happy. His clients tried to sue for their money back, but they couldn't, because lawsuits can make people unhappy.

In an interview with Matt after he won, he said that his life had been one long miserable success. Then Disney whisked him off.

For the rest of the world, things kept getting worse. Disney overtook China as the world's largest holder of US debt. In fact, China was in trouble. Its citizens wanted to be happy ever after too, and they sunk trillions into the lottery.

When Matt won, I quit my job. I'd never liked my job anyway. I didn't need that kind of misery. I heard a rumour that Madeleine was living at Versailles, so I made my way to France.

I found a hostel in Paris and stayed there for a week. That was all the money I had and I moved to the street. Paris looked better than it ever had, but the people were in rough shape. I found out from a guy, Pierre who was a hired actor for Disney, that Madeleine liked to visit the city. Disney had an entire staff of fake Parisians whose job was to make sure she only had happy experiences there.

When she came into town, the real citizens of Paris were swept into holding pens and replaced by actors. In Madeleine's Paris everyone was friendly and fair. The vendors in Madeleine's Paris gave her a discount parce-que elle était si jolie and restaurants gave her hors d'ouevres and desserts on the house.

Pierre told me Disney ran a pretty tight ship, but it wasn't that tight. He was able to get me an acting gig as a busboy at a restaurant Madeleine frequented.

I'd cut my hair, and I'd lost a few pounds, but Madeleine recognized me right away.

"Hey, come over here," she said.

HAPPILY EVER AFTER

"Hey Madeleine," I said.

"What are you doing here?"

"I came looking for you. I still love you Madeleine. I needed to see you. I've tried to write, but Disney keeps sending the letters back."

Madeleine laughed. "It's good to see you. I'm glad you're okay," she said and then she and her date got up and walked out of the restaurant. I followed them.

"I'm not okay Madeleine. Nobody is. Except you and some asshole who used his clients' money to win the second lottery. The world's going to hell Madeleine," I said.

Then two guys grabbed me and dragged me into the kitchen. They roughed me up a bit and then they put me on a plane to Disney World in Orlando. They put a chip in my ankle and I get fifty thousand volts through my body if I try to leave the cotton candy stall. I'm stuck in there all day every day. I make cotton candy Disney characters. At first I was terrible at it. You couldn't tell who any of them were supposed to be. I've gotten pretty good, though. Donald Duck is my best one.

On our second date, I told Madeleine that I'd do anything to see that she was happy. Now I know better.

Madagascar

I never liked Leonard. He lived next door to me growing up and my mom always went on about him. She'd ask me why I couldn't be more like him, even though Leonard was a year younger than me and a head shorter and I could take him in a fight.

Now Leonard's been blamed for the deaths of 312 people and I feel sorry for him.

The headlines said that Leonard high-jacked a plane, but he was the pilot, so really he commandeered it. He called me a month before he did it. I saw his name come up on the call display, but I answered it anyway.

"Man, I'm dying," he said. "They give me six weeks or something like that."

"Shit man. We'll have to get together for a beer before that then," I said.

Leonard had an idea on how he wanted to go out. He wanted to take a plane full of commuters and reroute them to Madagascar.

"Why Madagascar?"

"Because it's a unique ecosystem. Did you know that eighty percent of the fauna and ninety percent of the flora in Madagascar aren't found anywhere else in the world? And those people need to get away. Have you ever been on a weekday commuter flight? I could take them to the Galapagos, but there's nowhere to land a plane that size there. Besides, there's more to do in Madagascar," he said.

Personally I could've thought of some people worthier of getting away than a bunch of businessmen on a Monday morning flight, but it wasn't my plane, and I didn't figure Leonard would actually do it. Then one morning he commandeered a flight from Toronto to New York. He dropped a few bills on the fuelling crew to make sure the tank had enough gas to get to Madagascar and then he took off.

Leonard cut radio contact half an hour after takeoff. According to the flight log he was afraid somebody would try to talk him out of it. The plane went over New York and then out over the east coast of the US and into the Atlantic. Once it was over the Atlantic, homeland security decided they couldn't risk the plane coming back and crashing into something important, so they shot it down.

There were 312 people on board and they all died. Leonard got the blame. The guy didn't even get a funeral. The United States wouldn't repatriate the body to Canada and the Canadian government said they didn't want it back anyway.

My mom called me after she saw it on the news. "I was always glad you weren't like Leonard, you know. Growing up he always seemed a little off to me," she said.

That's when I really started to feel sorry for him. Even my mom turned against him. And the poor guy just wanted to take some people to Madagascar before he died.

Graham Ericsson Dies

Graham Ericsson died. I sat across from him on the ferry over the River Styx. It wasn't a coincidence that we were on the same ferry. I read his obituary in The New York Times and knew he'd be coming.

Graham was a writer. He wrote fifteen novels. The last thirteen of them were bestsellers. They're all the same. I guess it took people a while to appreciate his stuff. When I say they're the same I mean they're word for word the same. The only difference between the books is the characters' names.

It's hard to believe, but nobody noticed. Not even the critics. When Graham's third book came out, the reviewers said that he had arrived. His third book is still his most highly regarded, although there are some critics who claim that his last book was his best.

The New York Times called his last book, "a tour de force." They said that Graham Ericsson was, "possibly the English language's most consistent author. He does it time and again." I suppose they were technically right.

Me and Lefty had a bet going on whether or not Graham knew he was writing the same book over and over. I said he knew. Lefty said no way.

Benson, who was responsible for watching Graham while Graham was alive, swore that the guy sweated every word.

"It's fucking hilarious. The son of a bitch, he drafts and redrafts. He almost wound up with an extra sentence in chapter twelve of his second novel, but the editor cut it. And in his fourteenth book, the editor didn't like the ending and asked Graham to change it. Graham rewrote it six times and all six endings were terrible. In the end the editor gave up and they used the same ending they'd used for the previous thirteen books."

You can never believe the shit Benson says, though. According to people who knew Benson when he was alive, you couldn't believe him then either.

It's hard enough to buy that nobody else noticed that Graham wrote and published the same book fifteen times, but that Graham never noticed, that's too much.

It is true that nobody else noticed, though. If you go into a bookstore and ask, the salespeople all have an opinion on his best and his worst book. Usually they go with the critics and say the third book, but not always. Some say his last book. The pretentious ones say his first book, and a few have a particular favourite.

Graham sold millions of books. His writing was translated into dozens of languages. At some point, somebody must have laid his books side by side. At the very least, somebody in a bookstore must have read the first couple of pages of a few of his books. It kills me that the fucker pulled it off.

I was by myself on the ferry. Lefty hasn't been dead as long as I have. He still finds it creepy riding with all the newbies, but I like it. The river's pretty, and the ferry's the only place around where you can get a decent hotdog.

GRAHAM ERICSSON DIES

The ferry's not the gondola with the pole that you usually see in movies and stuff. It's a modern boat with three decks, including one for cars. The ride takes about forty-five minutes each way. If you sit up on the top deck, you get a good view. Graham was on the top deck. I went over to him.

"Hey, you're Graham Ericsson, aren't you," I said.

"Yes I am."

"Settle something for me. Was it intentional?"

"Was what intentional?"

"Your work. Was it intentional?"

"I'm not sure what you mean."

"Your books are all the same," I said.

"Look, if you're not a fan of my work …"

"How the fuck did you pull it off? I mean I know you changed the names each time, but still. Fifteen books. How on Earth did you manage it?"

Graham got up and moved seats. He looked uncomfortable. Most people look uncomfortable their first time on the Styx, but Graham more so. He knew.

I waited until he sat down again and then I pulled my knapsack out from under the bench and went after him. The knapsack had copies of all fifteen of Graham's books. They were all the same edition, except for the last book. You could overlay the first page or the last page of any two books and you could see that they were the same. The pages were slightly staggered as you went through because of the different names, and because sometimes he threw in a line break here or there.

The longest book is the seventh, because the protagonist is Alouicious Rosenthal MacStravick and he's always referred to by all three names at once. The shortest is the eighth book because all the characters are known by single letters. You wouldn't think it would make that much of a difference, but the seventh book is forty-two pages longer than the eighth.

I sat down on Graham's left.

"What do you want?" he said.

I was all ready to stick it to him. I unzipped my knapsack and pulled out Graham's first book. His lower lip quivered. He had a look in his eyes that I'd never seen before. I had a feeling like if I pulled out the other fourteen books and showed him, that it would kill him. Again. It's rare, but it's been known to happen.

"I was just hoping I could have your autograph," I said.

"Yeah, sure," he said. He took a pen out of his hip pocket and signed the inside of the front cover. He wrote his name and that was it. He didn't ask who to make it out to or anything. I put the book back in my knapsack. I went and got a hotdog and a coke and let the poor bastard be.

It doesn't mean that Benson's not full of shit, but I settled up with Lefty as soon as we docked.

Marla

One night I worked late. My wife was supposed to pick me up at nine. I came out of the building, walked across the mall to the turning circle and got into a car. It looked like our car, but it wasn't. It was winter and it was cold and snowy and the wind whipped the snow around. I had my head down and I guess I wasn't paying attention.

It was a woman behind the wheel of the car. She was ten years older than me, maybe fifteen. She was still pretty though.

"Hi dear," she said and then she drove off. I didn't say anything.

We went to a really nice place near downtown, half a block from the canal. It was a lot nicer than the townhouse in the suburbs that I shared with Tammy.

The woman pulled the car into the garage and went into the house. I followed her. She took off her coat and boots and went upstairs. She glanced at me a couple of times but she didn't take a good look.

I figured I should say something to her, or call Tammy and explain. Probably I should do both. I should at least do something. I went into the kitchen.

I was hungry so I went through the fridge and the freezer. There was cookie dough ice cream in the freezer. I went through the cupboards and found a bowl and a spoon and had some. Afterwards I washed the bowl and the spoon and put them away.

The woman didn't come back downstairs. I wandered around the house. The place was huge. In the end I slept in the guest bedroom on the first floor because I didn't want to disturb anything. If the woman's husband came home in the middle of the night, I didn't want to be in bed next to her.

Her husband didn't come home. Tammy didn't call me and I didn't call Tammy.

In the morning I showered and went to work like everything was normal. I walked. The wind and snow had let up. The walk took me fifteen minutes. It was a nice way to start the day. It was better than forty-five minutes in traffic.

At the end of the day I walked back to the woman's house. I got there at the same time she did. It didn't seem to surprise her that I was there.

I stayed in the guest room again that night. In the morning I showered and walked to work, and in the afternoon I walked back again. When I got there the woman handed me a key. I put it on my ring.

Sleeping in the guest bedroom and walking to and from work became my new routine. A few times I thought that I should call Tammy, but I could never figure out how to explain why I hadn't called before.

The woman's name was Marla. Mostly Marla and I led separate lives. A couple of times a week we'd have dinner. Marla was a terrible cook, so I made the dinners. One night, about a month after

MARLA

I'd moved in, we had too much wine with dinner and we slept together.

Marla fucked me. It was violent. Marla was pretty but she lacked youth. She was at an age where fat wasn't attractive anymore, so she'd lost it all. She was nothing but bone and sinew. She twisted and coiled and pounded and it was great, but afterwards there was nothing to lie against. We were in bed and her elbow was in my ribs and her knee was in my thigh.

"I don't make that much," I said.

"Huh?"

"I can't afford this place Marla. Christ, I probably can't even afford the property taxes on this place."

"So?"

"So I …"

"Look. Stan works the same shitty job you do only he's twenty years older than you. At least at your age there's still hope. I make plenty of money, so don't worry," she said.

"Okay."

It wasn't a bad deal. Mostly Marla left me to do my own thing. Every now and then she expected a good fuck, but she was hardly insatiable.

She and Stan had one kid, a daughter Liz, who was studying at UBC. Liz had her own bedroom, but she didn't come home to visit. Her room was decorated like she was still ten years old. It was full of stuffed animals and show jumping medals.

There was a recent picture of Liz in the living room on top of the piano. Liz wasn't a ten year old with stuffed animals. She was twenty and she was hot as hell. She was thick, but not overweight. She had an athlete's thighs. When I knew Marla wouldn't be around, I'd take Liz's picture into her bedroom and jerk off on her bed. Mostly those were the best orgasms I've ever had.

Then one day Marla announced that Liz was coming home to visit. It was the end of May. Liz hadn't come home at Christmas, or at reading week, or at Easter, or at the end of the term. She called on a Tuesday and said she'd be home Thursday morning. Marla was really excited.

"What about Stan?" I said.

"What about Stan? Liz knows that her father's a loser. It'll be fine."

That night Marla insisted on fucking. I didn't want to. I had a tough time getting hard. I wanted Liz and not Marla. Afterwards, I lay awake and thought about Liz and when I was sure Marla was asleep I took Liz's picture to her room and jerked off.

The next morning I packed a bag and took it to work. At the end of the day I stood out by the turning circle where people get picked up and dropped off.

I thought about Tammy for the first time in months. I thought about calling her, but then she'd never called me. She could have tracked me down no problem. I hadn't changed jobs or phone numbers. Probably she was happier without me. Even if she wasn't, it was too late for that. Tammy'd have somebody new by now. People were attracted to Tammy.

I found a hotel for the night. I ate in a restaurant down the street. It felt good to be on my own.

MARLA

In the morning I called in sick to work. I spent the day looking for an apartment. I found one right downtown, available immediately. It wasn't that nice, but the location was good and the rent was cheap. I signed the lease before I left and I moved in that night.

I didn't have any furniture or anything. I was thirty-six and everything that was mine fit in a suitcase. I slept on the floor with some clothes piled under my head. I slept better than I could ever remember having slept.

Still, I got a mattress and some pillows and a couch and a TV. You need something to keep you occupied and you can only sleep on the floor for so long. Tammy still hasn't called. Marla hasn't called either. Sometimes I think about calling one of them, but I never do.

Sapiens Versus Neanderthalensis

It's true that only people have souls, but it turns out there's more to the story. There are these little wisps that populate the afterlife. They're small and stooped and they do the menial jobs like clean the bathrooms. Some of the more advanced ones get to hold doors or push buttons on elevators.

When I got here, somebody explained it all to me. The wisps are proto-souls. The really primitive ones are australopithecus. They're not good for much. Then there's homo habilis and after that homo erectus. Some of the homo erectus are almost useful. Above all of them, there's us.

"What about the Neanderthals?" I said. Most people get around to that question sooner or later.

There aren't any Neanderthals in the afterlife because they lost. It was close for about a thousand years, but in the end we kicked their asses so we got in. God spent millennia trying to get what he wanted in an apex creature, but he kept coming back to two different designs. He put the two different designs on the Earth and let them fight it out. Souls to the winner.

It turns out Limbo's real, or it was real. That's where all the dead humans and Neanderthals were held until we won. After we won the Neanderthals blew away into the ether and we got the afterlife.

That's what we'd assumed anyway. Now it's not so sure. The Neanderthals were cagey fuckers. When they saw the pictorials on the wall, they interbred. The species died out, but there are traces of it flowing through a lot of people. The traces are remote. Nobody here can follow their family tree to a Neanderthal. We're people, homo sapiens. And we're in danger.

There's talk on Earth of recreating Neanderthals using their genome and existing DNA strands in modern people. If that happens, we're all screwed. Just one living Neanderthal means the war's back on and we're back to Limbo.

If that happens, these filthy little pseudo souls will run the place and they'll wreck it. Supposedly you should've seen the afterlife when we got here. Supposedly it was full of lean-tos and fire pits and shit was strewn everywhere.

That's not the real danger, though. The real danger is that the Neanderthals will become a viable population. If that happens, they could win or even create a new crossbreed that god likes better.

It's not inconceivable. Neanderthals are fertile at a younger age than people and their metabolisms are made for high calorie first world diets. Popular opinion is that Neanderthals were dumber than us, but their brains were bigger and nobody truly knows. Some of the really old souls claim they knew Neanderthals when they were alive, but thirty thousand years will make the best memories hazy and they can't seem to agree on much about them.

SAPIENS VERSUS NEANDERTHALENSIS

All this genetic experimentation might seem like a good idea. Hell, it might even be good for the Earth. But it's not good for us. We might not win so easily the second time round. Think about it. Neanderthals embedded themselves in our bodies. Maybe they didn't think about it, but maybe they saw this day coming. If that's the case then it means they're actually smarter than us and we're all doomed.

Kissing

We were playing kissing tag at recess, where the girls had to kiss the boys and Erica kissed me on the lips. She was chasing me and I tried to lose her by jumping over the bottom of the slide. I tripped and banged my shin on the edge of the slide and fell in the sand. Erica jumped on top of me and kissed me right on the lips. It was gross, but after it was all I could think about.

The slide left a big bruise on my shin and I could barely walk. I was mad at Erica. Kissing tag was her idea in the first place. I never liked Erica anyway. I had a dream that night. It started with Erica chasing me and I tripped on the slide again and she kissed me on the lips again. But then we kept kissing.

We played kissing tag at school once in awhile. I tried hard not to get kissed by the other girls. Erica has brown, curly hair that bounces when she runs and her lips are redder than the other girls and I think she might need a bra soon. Sherry's the only girl in our class who wears a bra, but Sherry's not pretty.

After Erica kissed me on the lips, I tried to get caught by her when we played kissing tag. I tried not to look like I was trying to get caught though.

The last time we played, I got Erica to chase me around to the front of the school, on the other side from the playground, where we're not supposed to go. I tripped and fell by the flowerbed. I fell there on purpose, because girls like flowers, but I still twisted my ankle when I did it.

Erica kissed me on the knee and went to run off. That was no good, so I tripped her onto the grass.

"I want to be your boyfriend," I said. "But you have to promise not to tell anyone."

"I don't want a boyfriend," Erica said, but she kissed me on the lips.

I kissed her back. I was lying beside her while we kissed and I could feel her chest. That's how I know she's going to need a bra soon.

We got caught by Mrs Randall. Mrs Randall was our principal. She came up and stood over us and cleared her throat really loudly. She had a cigarette in her hand. That explained why she smelled gross up close. "I want both of you to go to my office now. Wait there for me," she said.

Mrs Randall took a drag on her cigarette and threw the butt into the flowerbed. Then she followed me and Erica inside.

We went into Mrs Randall's office. Mrs Randall sat down behind her desk. Erica and I stood in front of it.

"Now. I would very much like it if the two of you would tell me what was going on," Mrs Randall said.

"Nothing," I said.

"That was most certainly not nothing. Why were you out of the school yard?"

"We were playing kissing tag and Jimmy ran around there. And then he tripped and I caught him," Erica said.

"Really?"

KISSING

"Yes Mrs Randall," I said.

"First of all, you should know that kissing tag is not an appropriate game for children your age. And second of all, what I saw was more than kissing tag."

"It wasn't. You can ask anyone," Erica said.

Mrs Randall asked everyone including my best friend Tom. My best friend Tom told her that I had a crush on Erica and that I'd bragged to him about kissing her.

"Why'd you have to tell her that?" I said to Tom.

"Because it's gross. You're the one who always insists that we play kissing tag anyway. None of the other guys like it," Tom said.

"Then why do they play?" I said.

Our teacher talked to our class about how kissing and touching was not appropriate for children our age. She told us that kissing tag was not a good game to play, and Mrs Randall sent home a note to our parents about it.

"You shouldn't be thinking about those sorts of things at your age," my parents said.

"You're too young to like girls," my older sister said.

At school, the guys were pissed off at me. I got into a fight with Tom at lunch and another one with Hussein at afternoon recess and Mrs Randall suspended me for two days. Even after, the guys didn't talk to me very much for a while.

Neither did Erica. That was okay, though, because I didn't really like Erica. I always felt funny when she got close to me.

We don't play kissing tag anymore. Mrs Randall said the school would have a zero tolerance policy towards kissing tag.

That's okay too, because I don't like kissing tag either, even though I lie in bed at night sometimes and I think about playing it and Erica catches me. But I don't like kissing tag and I don't know why I think about it.

Historical Accuracy

Elise Dupont wrote a history of Rome from its founding to Augustus' death. It's forty-eight volumes of over a thousand pages each. It makes Edward Gibbon look lazy, which is lucky, because nowadays nobody wants to read that much. They don't even read Gibbon.

It's lucky because everything Elise Dupont wrote is right, every detail. It's hard to believe, because the ancient sources are such bullshit. We carefully chose Tacitus, Livy, Seutonius and Plutarch because they were out of their minds. We let Cicero through because he was such a self-absorbed whiner, and everyone knows Julius Caesar had an agenda.

Where it was necessary, we made sure of some strategic edits and omissions by the monks and presto, nobody ever needed to know.

A lot of people have been sniffing around for a long time. All those renaissance princelings and then the Americans. Ancient Rome's something of an obsession. A few people got wound up whenever a new book came out. There was a lot of hand wringing over Edward Gibbon because he got a couple of things right, but he made up for it by being wrong about almost everything else.

Most of us weren't worried, though. We made sure the truth was pretty murky.

Then along comes this Elise Dupont bitch and she nails it. Fifty thousand pages and the only thing she got wrong were the earrings Cleopatra had on when she died. Big whoop.

There are a couple of people clinging to those earrings like a plank off a sinking ship. "The butterfly effect," they say. As if, had Cleopatra worn hoops, it would have set off a chain reaction that would have led to Augustus' overthrow, the Republic would've been preserved, the Goths wouldn't have sacked Rome and everybody would speak Latin.

The hope is that Elise Dupont's work doesn't catch on. So far it hasn't. She's been ridiculed by all the serious Roman scholars. The best that's been said about her work is "implausible." That's good, but there are rumours she's planning an abridged version that regular people might actually read. There's also talk of a series of movies. Obviously they'll change some stuff, but they might popularize her version of what happened.

That would be disaster. Two thousand years isn't enough time for the dust to settle on a lot of the shit that went on.

In the old days it was easier. If somebody got too close, we found an out of work arsonist. We took care of a lot when we got Alexandria. Once or twice a manuscript got through. When that happened we made sure it got into the hands of an appropriately religious monk. We could always rely on the monks to make some creative edits.

Now with technology it's not so easy. On top of the arsonist, you need a computer expert to track down all the electronic copies and erase them. Even if we can make all that work, we don't know how

HISTORICAL ACCURACY

Elise Dupont figured it out. It looks like just dumb luck a lot of it. It's possible she couldn't even do it again.

Maybe she could though. Romulus and Augustus think we should assassinate her and then find someone to unearth ancient sources that are completely made up. Caesar says we should convince her to print a retraction and Cicero just keeps talking about the goddamned Catiline Conspiracy.

Personally I'm sick of it. Two thousand years of scheming and paranoia's too much. Sure it won't be flattering for me. Cato keeps pointing out that right now nobody even knows who I am and do I want them to find out like that. The truth is I don't, but there are other people who will get it worse than me and maybe I can finally get some rest.

The Wrong Side of the Bed

The first time I woke up on the wrong side of the bed I didn't say anything, because I wasn't sure. I thought maybe I'd fallen asleep on that side and I'd just forgotten.

I was crabby all day though. My boss walked by my cubicle and I was hitting my keyboard with the phone receiver because the phone receiver wasn't working. "Somebody got up on the wrong side of the bed," he said. It happened again at the coffee shop in the afternoon. The milk jug was empty. I bounced it off the counter and some smartass behind me said it.

I woke up on the wrong side of the bed again two mornings later and then each of the two mornings after that. I couldn't understand how it happened. It made me jumpy. The third morning I dropped the toothpaste tube into the toilet and I pulled it out and threw it across the bathroom. Kelly was fixing her hair in the mirror. I just missed her head.

"Fuck. Somebody woke up on the wrong side of the bed," she said.

"So you've noticed it too," I said.

"What?"

"That we're waking up on the wrong sides of the bed."

"It's too early in the morning."

"You haven't noticed that I keep waking up on your side of the bed?" I said.

"No. Obviously you're not crowding me or anything."

"That's because you're on my side of the bed."

"I am? Do you want to switch sides? I really don't care which side of the bed I sleep on."

"What? No. I." I let it drop, but it kept happening. I went to bed on my side of the bed, but woke up on Kelly's side. Kelly insisted she didn't notice, but it was happening almost every night. How could she not notice? I started to suspect that she was fucking with me.

One night I set the alarm for four in the morning to see if I could catch her. It scared the shit out of both of us when it went off. Kelly was in the middle of the bed, but I was still on my side. I sat up in bed and waited until it was time to go to work. Kelly leaned her head against my chest and slept. Nothing happened.

I set the alarm for four again the next night and Kelly didn't cuddle up to me. She said, "What the fuck?" and then she rolled over and went back to sleep on her side.

The next night I didn't set the alarm and I woke up on the wrong side of the bed again. My face was up against the headboard. My left leg was off the bed and my ass hurt. Kelly was curled up peacefully with her head on my pillow.

"We're on the wrong sides again," I said.

"Are we onto this again?"

"I sleep on that side."

"I don't understand what you're talking about."

THE WRONG SIDE OF THE BED

"Look. That's my book on that bedside table. It's my watch too," I said.

She took them off the night table and handed them to me. "Is that better?" she said, but it wasn't.

I set the alarm again. This time I set it for four-thirty. Still nothing. The next night I set the alarm for quarter-to-five, but Kelly turned it off. I woke up facing the bottom of the bed with my feet hooked into the headboard and a pillow over my head. I had a wicked cramp in my left thigh. I got up and shook Kelly awake.

"Okay. What the fuck is going on?" I said.

Kelly said that nothing was going on. We had a huge fight and Kelly called me that afternoon to tell me that she was going to stay at her sister's for the night.

That was fine with me. I grabbed a baseball bat and put it on Kelly's pillow. I sat up in bed and drank coffee until three in the morning. Then I lay down and pretended to be asleep. At some point I actually fell asleep.

I woke up at five and there were ropes around my wrists and ankles, tied to the bed frame and eight little men with a baseball bat were on my chest. The men were really little, maybe eight or ten inches. I felt like I was in Gulliver's Travels.

I freaked out when I saw the little men. I tried to sit up, but they'd tied the ropes well. "You little fuckers!" I said.

"Hey, he's awake," one of them said and then they hit me in the chest with the baseball bat.

"Oops," another one said.

"We should get out of here."

"It's too late. He knows now. We'll have to silence him before he can tell anybody."

"They won't believe him anyway. Remember that last poor shit, how they came and took him away?"

"Still."

"Okay, what the fuck is going on?" I said.

"He's talking to us."

"It sounds like it. We're breaking you up. You're not good enough for her," one of them said.

"What do you care?" I said.

"Shut up. You're annoying. Go back to sleep."

I got really pissed and I managed to get my right arm free. I ripped the bat out of their hands and threw it across the room.

"Shit," one of them said.

I grabbed the one who'd told me to go back to sleep and threatened to bite his head off if they didn't let me go. One of them ran up my face and tried to ram himself into my nostril. I threw the first guy across the room and undid my other arm. The first guy bounced off the wall and landed on the floor.

I sat up and undid the ropes around my legs and the little men ran and got the bat.

"Come on you fuckers," I said. They swung the bat and I grabbed the top of it. I bent over and picked one of them up and threatened again to kill him.

They got the bat free and swung it into my shins and I bit the one guy's head clean off. Blood spurted everywhere. They hit me in the shins a second time and I collapsed backwards onto the bed. They jumped up. They could really jump. They grabbed a pillow and tried to smother me with it. I managed to throw them off again. One of them landed on the floor and I got up and stomped on his head. I was growling and snarling and I was going to kill them all and Kelly came in.

That was it for Kelly and me. She packed some clothes and left. The other six guys ran for cover under the bed. My hair was all over the place and my chest and face were covered in blood.

"Jesus Christ, what's wrong with you?" Kelly said and then she walked out. She sent her brother and sister for the rest of her stuff. It sucks, because Kelly really was too good for me. She was smarter and better looking and had a better job than me, but at least I sleep better at night now.

The Meek

I got called in for psychological testing. The first day it was all multiple choice questions. There were four thousand of them. The rest of the week was short answers. They let me go for the weekend. The second week was all essay questions. Weeks three and four were interviews and I was hooked up to machines that monitored my heart rate and brainwave activity.

We all had to do it. They brought us in a city at a time. A couple of the really big cities like New York and Tokyo and Mumbai and Mexico had to be done in more than one round, but for the most part that's how they did it.

They tested me for four weeks, but Ahmed said his testing only lasted two days and my wife Alicia's testing took a week. She said she didn't know whether that was good or bad.

After the testing was done, we were all rounded up to go through security. Alicia breezed through even though she had shampoo and lipstick and vodka and all kinds of shit in her bag that she wasn't allowed, but they pulled me out of the line. They put me in a room with incandescent lights and big men and one of the psychologists who'd done my testing.

They handed me a folder and said it had my test scores in it. "Your score is a little low," the psychologist said. "Not by much. Just five points as you can see if you look." I studied the papers in the folder and tried to see how it was. "Still, I'm afraid that means we can't let you on. This isn't easy, but as you know, we don't have room for everybody and someone has to get left behind."

"You let Alicia through. How can you let her through, but not her husband?"

"Alicia is not you. Her scores were higher than yours."

We went back and forth for half an hour and then they threw me out and I was stuck on Earth. About a third of us got stuck on Earth. We were the ones who didn't kick up enough of a fuss. Apparently the security screening was the final test. Some people who bombed the rest of it got through.

Jared got through. The rumour was he had one of the lowest scores in the entire world, but they told him to go home and he wouldn't. They beat him for four hours and he wouldn't leave and he didn't cry. Not one tear and they let him on. Naseen jumped the gates and punched the first guy who tried to stop him and they let him on. If I'd thought of something like that I probably would have gotten on too.

Instead I'm stuck on Earth. The Earth is a mess, which I guess is how it was always supposed to be. There's a two thousand year old copy of the Sermon on the Mount that reads: "Cursed are the meek, for they shall inherit the Earth when we are done with it." Several experts have authenticated it. They said that the better known phrasing was a fifth century forgery invented to help keep the peasants in line.

There are three billion of us here going about our business as usual. Most people are still getting up and going to work each morning whether or not they still have jobs. I say we need to get organized. We need to make sure of our food supply and we need to build some rockets to get off of this planet. The new world is bigger than Earth. There's no way it can't hold all of us.

The only problem is they made sure none of the astrophysicists got left behind, and they didn't leave any rockets or blueprints on which to base new ones. At this point we couldn't recreate the Challenger series.

It doesn't much matter, anyway. Everyone seems to realize we need leaders, but nobody wants the job. I talk to people and they say, "You should organize something," but even if I wanted to, I'd need to be able to reach a wide enough audience.

So far, I can't. I've been writing editorials on the subject for weeks, but the online media is still controlled remotely by the others and they refuse to publish me.

It's so frustrating that I want to cry. We need a revolution. There are moments, late at night when I'm alone, where I think I can lead it, but in the morning I go to work and I look around and I think about how it would be if people wouldn't follow me.

I've given up going to church, though. The pastors are all gone anyway, but the churches are still there. A lot of people go into them to pray, but not me. Blessed are the meek. Two thousand years they conned us.

Broadway

Rod exploded in front of the John Golden Theatre in Midtown, right after the doors opened to let people in. Rod was with a date. According to her, when the line-up started moving he stood there for a second looking queasy and then blam. Our parents started a foundation in his name.

Rod didn't just collapse or melt or fall to pieces. He really exploded. His spleen wound up on the side of the theatre twenty yards away. Most of him wound up on his date. She was covered in Rod's insides. I can't remember her name. Melissa I think. She's not involved with the foundation.

Rod was my little brother. Two years younger than me. He was thirty-three when he exploded. He had a rare condition. Most doctors say it doesn't exist, but there are a few who insist it does. There's a lot written about it on the internet. According to the internet it's usually the result of trauma, but in Rod's case, it looks like trauma wasn't a factor.

Rod was tall and gangly. Even as a baby. When he was twelve he got to be taller than me and he stayed that way. He had no control over his limbs though. He'd trip over himself going upstairs to use the bathroom.

"He just has to grow into himself," my mom said, but he stayed that way.

He was the same intellectually. He wasn't stupid, he just never thought about anything or did anything. He worked part-time at Blockbuster for ten years after high school and lived with our parents.

"He just has to grow into himself," my mom said.

Then he did. He turned thirty and he started to get coordinated. He found a full-time job. He got his own place and went to university nights.

It didn't stop there. Rod kept getting better at stuff. He got promoted three times in five months and he finished an honours degree in engineering and a Masters in physics in one year of night school. Columbia accepted him to a PhD program and he moved to New York.

Rod did his PhD in another year and was the star of Columbia's hockey team at the same time. When he was twenty-nine, he could barely stand up on skates.

He got really bad migraines though and joint and back pain.

"What do you expect? You're working twenty hours a day," I said.

"I'm not. I swear I'm not. You wouldn't believe, but I get eight hours sleep every night. All this stuff I do, it's easy. I don't know why. It's like I've got purpose all of a sudden and everything has just clicked into place," he said.

"That's great, but if you're getting pain so bad it makes you cry, you need to go see a doctor."

"Yeah."

I was never close with Rod, but he tried to make us be. He called me three or four times a week. He tried to explain to me how it was for him. I didn't get it, but I talked him into seeing a doctor who sent him to a bunch of doctors.

The doctors did all kinds of tests and they couldn't find anything wrong with Rod. Except for one quack who said he knew exactly what it was.

"It's called delayed internal growth," he said. "In 99.99% of cases it's fine. It's even healthy. The inner person catches up with the body. Once in a very rare while though, the inner person doesn't know when to stop growing. It outgrows the body and then the body just explodes. I'm afraid there's no treatment. I'm sorry."

"The guy's full of shit," I said.

"No, he's right," Rod said. "It fits perfectly. I understand the world in a way I never did before, in a way I don't think most people ever do. I hope that doesn't sound arrogant. It's …"

The quack's on the foundation's board.

After the diagnosis, Rod started to write a treatise. On everything. It wasn't an encyclopaedia. It was almost prophetic. Maybe it was prophetic. He was three hundred pages into his treatise when he blew up on Broadway.

Rod knew he was dying so he'd done a will. In it he asked that I finish his treatise as best I could.

My parents started the foundation in Rod's name. I read a couple of pages of his treatise and then I burned it. It's not much of a way to treat your younger brother's legacy, but I don't want to learn too much from him. Nobody knows exactly what caused Rod to explode and I don't want to be next.

I may be missing the greatest opportunity in the history of mankind, but better that than exploding on a busy street in Manhattan. Especially all over a date. A person doesn't forget a thing like that.

Creative

I killed this guy for god. It wasn't a crusade or righteous vengeance or anything. And I didn't kill him in god's name. I was having lunch at McDonald's and god came and sat at my table.

"I want to hire you," he said and then he went and ordered a Double Big Mac meal with a large fries and a large coke.

God said he was hiring me on behalf of the devil as well, but I never met the devil. God looked sort of like Morgan Freeman.

"I always pictured you more as George Burns," I told him and he scowled.

"You know Chuck Wolanski?" god said.

"The writer?"

"I need him killed."

"What for?"

"Do I need to give a reason? Do you ask your mortal clients why they want somebody killed?"

"No, but what can I say, I'm curious," I said.

"Fine. Name a writer, a musician, a TV show, anything at all creative that gets better with age."

"Chuck Wolanski."

"Exactly. Name somebody else. They get more polished, but the creative spark fades. They recycle the same ideas. They try new ideas that aren't any good. The first major work is almost always the best. Sometimes I let them have one at the end, but otherwise it's a steady downhill.

"Not Chuck. Nooo. He's on his second TV series and it gets better with each episode. Same thing with his novels. His first novel was barely legible and completely pointless. I don't know how in the hell he got it published. But his latest novel has won awards all over the world and deserved to. And he's only forty-eight. Given medicine these days he could conceivably keep this up for another fifty years. Maybe longer. I've looked at the results of his physicals. The man's in good shape for somebody half his age. With fifty years he could eclipse the entire rest of humanity."

I thought about it for a bit. I watched Chuck's TV show and I'd read his latest novel. His stuff was brilliant. I tried to come up with somebody else who had gotten better with age. "What about Bruce Springsteen?" I said. "He didn't really find his stride until the mid-eighties."

God laughed. Then he hired me for twelve hundred bucks US and a twenty-five year old Sony Walkman with a blank tape in it. The tape had one song on it recorded over and over for ninety minutes: Bruce Springsteen's Growin' Up. The song's just over three minutes long. God got it onto the tape twenty-nine times by wrapping one recording around from the first side to the second.

"How about an iPod?" I said when god handed me the Walkman.

"What's an iPod?"

To be honest, god wasn't the most rewarding client I've ever had. For starters, twelve hundred US is awfully cheap for a hit these days. And god only actually gave me six hundred. He said that was his half and the devil would pay the other half once the job was finished. Then he popped up all the time to see how things were going and to make sure I was listening to the tape he'd given me.

Chuck's TV show was at a critical plot point and rumour had it he was halfway through a new novel, so I dragged my feet on the killing. God could tell.

"If you don't hurry up, I'll go find somebody else who's interested in doing god's work," he said.

I shot Chuck going into a Barnes and Noble in upstate New York. God was there. He was distracting. I listened to the walkman and tried to ignore him, but he kept looking over top of the rifle and saying, "What was wrong with that shot?"

I took a mediocre shot just to shut god up, and I missed. That was the first time since ninety-eight that I'd missed. People screamed and ducked and then they looked in our direction. God was scared and he split. I took a second shot and got Chuck right through the heart.

Sometimes I regret it. For one thing, Chuck's show has gone to hell without him. They've replaced him with a team of writers and none of them can write for shit. For another thing, it's been six months and I still haven't heard from god or the devil about the six hundred they still owe me. It's crossed my mind that god was testing me and that I wasn't actually supposed to kill Chuck, but I don't think so. God was pretty pushy about it. Besides, as good as Chuck's TV show and novels were, everyone's got to eat. I can't afford to get a reputation as a guy who doesn't follow through on a job.

Forget the Alamo

Every morning Davy Crockett comes in and yells "remember that place during the war for Texan independence where the Mexicans killed everybody." He says it just like that to drag it out and really rub it in.

It's not even the real Davy Crockett. It's just some guy who played him on Broadway in the fifties.

I was at the Alamo. Not when the Mexicans captured it. Three days before the battle, Commander Travis sent me out to get reinforcements. I was fourteen.

The night after I left I was in this saloon and there was this woman named Claire. Claire bought me a few drinks and took me to her room.

I completely forgot about the Alamo. I spent the next week in Claire's room drunk and fucking. It wasn't until someone came into town to announce that the fort had been sacked that I remembered I was supposed to be getting reinforcements.

Ever since then people have been saying, "remember that place during the war for Texan independence where the Mexicans killed everybody."

I preferred to forget again, but Claire was out of money and she moved on. I caught a train back east, but even there people kept saying it. I died in 1912 and people still hadn't shut up about it.

I can't figure out why. There was a lot worse shit happened over the years. The Alamo was like two hundred people.

Now that I'm dead, I spend every day in this bar. I drink until I can't remember the Alamo or my own name. And every morning this guy comes in and shouts at the top of his lungs, "remember that place during the war for Texan independence where the Mexicans killed everybody."

He looks just like Davy Crockett. It's uncanny. Except he dresses differently from how Davy Crockett did, at least when Davy was alive. Davy changed his look in the fifties after he saw the Disney miniseries about him.

It used to be Davy who came in every morning, but he's moved on somewhere else. I'd fight with Davy every morning.

"Remember. That's easy for you to say. You know they buried the ashes of everybody there in one coffin. That's how few people there were. And guess what. They put three names on the coffin and yours was one. So fuck off with your, 'remember that place during the war for Texan independence where the Mexicans killed everybody.' It's just about your fucking glorification," I'd shout at him.

Davy Crockett hated that. We often came to blows. He always kicked my ass, because I was ninety when I died and he was only forty-nine.

Now it's not even Davy Crockett who comes in. It's just some guy who looks like him. He comes in and shouts louder and more angrily than Davy ever did. I scream at him and I throw shit at him and he says, "relax pops. It's only a part."

FORGET THE ALAMO

To make it even worse, the bar recently introduced a policy that forbids them serving "persons who are obviously intoxicated." So now I can't forget my own name, let alone the Alamo, and I'm awake and sober when the guy who plays Davy Crockett comes in and yells, "remember that place during the war for Texan independence where the Mexicans killed everybody."

Today I was up a good hour before Davy came in. I had a couple of cups of coffee and I was pretty awake. Davy comes in every morning at nine on the dot, so this morning I got up at five to nine and locked the door. The fucker walked straight into it and broke his nose.

The bartender let him in and he shouted, "remember that place during the war for Texan independence where the Mexicans killed everybody," but his nose was broken and he had his hand over it and you could barely understand him.

Hagen

When I was a kid I had a stuffed bear named Hagen. I got him the Christmas I was two-and-a-half. My dad bought him at Ogilvie's, which isn't around any more. He said he pulled him off a shelf full of bears that looked just like Hagen.

I liked Hagen. At bedtime I took him up to my room and I hugged him and I told him he was Teddy, and he said no he wasn't. He said that was a lame name and he might be a teddy bear, but he didn't have to put up with that.

"I'm Baron Von, well, let's not. It's best to forget that. From now on I'm Hagen," he said.

I got out of bed and went and told my mom and she said, "that's nice dear, but it's bedtime." That's how Hagen and my mom remembered it anyway.

I took Hagen with me everywhere, because he didn't like being alone. My mom got sick of having him around. She asked me why I didn't just leave him on my bed like a normal kid. I tried explaining that Hagen wasn't normal, but Hagen wouldn't talk to her and she didn't believe me.

Hagen's favourite book was Winnie the Pooh. I made my mom read it over and over, until even I was sick of it. My mom kept trying to read us other stories, but Hagen didn't like the other stories.

"I'd like to have a hundred acre wood full of friends instead of these brain dead bits of fabric. Man, you know it didn't used to be like this," Hagen said.

I'm making Hagen sound self-absorbed, but he wasn't. He helped me sometimes when I had trouble with my homework and when I was sad and I cried he didn't care how hard I squeezed or if I got his fur all wet. He didn't even complain when I got angry and threw him at the walls, and he never belittled me or told me I was overreacting.

We used to pretend that we were pirates and that we were looking for buried treasure. Hagen would take something and hide it and then he'd draw up a map. The maps were hard to figure out, because Hagen could only hold the pencil between his paws and he wasn't very coordinated.

When we played, Hagen always mentioned how he had real buried treasure. "It's not quite buried, but it's hidden. It's locked away, anyway. It's really important stuff. Really important. When you're older I'll tell you and we can go and get it," Hagen said. I believed Hagen until I was nine. Then I started to notice that he never gave any details. I'd ask him where or what and he'd say that he'd tell me when I was older, but for now it was best if I didn't know too much.

My mom didn't like Hagen, but my parents mostly ignored him until I was ten. When I turned ten my mom said, "You're a big boy now. Ten year old boys don't play with teddy bears."

"He doesn't like to be called Teddy," I said.

My sister Tracy backed me up. "I'm twelve and I've still got stuffed animals on my bed," she said.

"Yes, but you're a girl. And you don't take them along everywhere. That's not normal," my mom said.

Tracy said to leave me alone. I never asked her, but I'm pretty sure Tracy knew that Hagen was real. Once or twice she came into my room while Hagen was talking or moving around. He always stopped what he was doing, but one time she got this look on her face.

After my mom told me I wasn't normal I turned up the pressure on Hagen about the treasure. "If you're telling the truth, I bet it'll get my mom off my back," I said. "And if it doesn't, we can just live off the treasure, right?"

"Look, I said it's important, okay. I'm not leaving something that important to a ten year old," Hagen said, and I stuffed him under the bed. That was the only night I didn't spend with him until he died, which happened when I was eleven and a half.

About a week before, Hagen started complaining about chest pains. Then one day he said, "How long do teddy bears live anyway?"

"I don't know. You're looking a little ratty, but a wash could fix that if you'd let me throw you in the machine. Winnie the Pooh was ninety-nine though, right and you're nowhere near that," I said.

"He wasn't ninety-nine. He would be when Christopher Robin was a hundred. That's not the same thing."

On Wednesday afternoon, I noticed Hagen's complexion wasn't so good. "You need a doctor. I guess you're a bear, so you need a vet," I said.

Hagen said he couldn't go to a vet. "I'm not a real bear. I'm a stuffed one," he said.

By the time I got home from school on Thursday, Hagen was dead. I bawled my eyes out and then I went downstairs and told my mom.

"Oh thank god," she said.

I told my mom I wanted to bury Hagen. "Maybe in the backyard, or maybe we should take him back to Germany and have the funeral there," I said.

"Why the hell would we go to Germany to bury a stuffed bear?" my mom said.

"Because that's where he was from. That's what the label says anyway."

"You can't even read the label anymore."

"Still," I said.

In the end my mom threw Hagen into the garbage in the kitchen with the leftover spaghetti. My dad said that clearly we weren't going to go to Germany, but what was the harm really in burying him under the maple tree in the backyard. Tracy agreed, but my mom said she didn't want to sentimentalize it. She said besides the bear looked fine to her. "Why don't you just keep the damn thing if you're that upset about it?"

My mom tried to hand Hagen to me, but I was afraid to touch him now that he was dead. He felt wrong.

Then out of the blue, twenty-five years later, this guy's at my door at ten o'clock on a Friday night. I'm alone watching Seinfeld reruns and he starts banging on the door to my place. I answer the door and there he is. He looks like he's in his late seventies, but skinny and pretty fit. "You had a teddy bear when you were a kid," he says in a

German accent. I say sure I did, who didn't and he says, "Yes, but yours was special. You still have yours."

"No I don't. I threw him out when I was eleven after the dog ripped his head off," I say.

"You're lying. I know. He was a sneaky one the Baron, and he was a survivor. I've been trying for thirty years to track down the Baron, and I've finally come to the right place. He was your bear," the man says.

"Who let you into the building?" I say and he shrugs and says it doesn't matter. He says what matters is that he's found the Baron after all this time. He says the Baron has some very valuable information. "I want to see him," he says and he fingers something in his pocket.

"I don't know who the Baron was, or what you're talking about, but this is weird. My teddy bear was named Hagen and I tossed him when I was eleven," I say.

"No, no, it's your bear. Hagen. See, Hagen's a German name. He told you to call him that, I bet. He talked. He must have told you about me and that's why you won't let me in," the man says.

I tell him fuck it come in and look around and he does. He goes through everything. He even finds it and he doesn't know what it is.

"What have you done with the Baron? You fool. You have no idea. Do you think he was just another talking bear? He was the only one who knew, you know," the man says. I shove him gently out the door and push it shut behind him.

Hagen told me about the treasure when he knew he was going to die. "I can't believe I'm telling an eleven year old," he said, and then he told me how there was a safe deposit box in a bank in Switzerland, just like in a movie.

When I was twenty I went to Europe for the summer with my girlfriend Lisa. We backpacked together for a month until Paris when she met a guy from Algeria who was staying in the same hostel as us. I woke up at four in the morning and Lisa was in his bed and I went to Switzerland on my own.

There wasn't much in Hagen's safe deposit box, just some stale Bazooka Joes and a little plastic ring like you used to get out of those vending machines in the front of the grocery stores. I chucked the Bazooka Joes, but I keep the ring in the top drawer of my dresser with my underwear.

I don't know if it's that teddy bears have a different sense of what's valuable or if it's that Hagen was full of shit. Either way I guess I should have told the old man, because he'll probably spend the rest of his life trying to track down Hagen's treasure.

The David

I'm the top selling dildo in the US and Canada. Not literally, obviously, but the top selling dildo in the US and Canada is based on my penis. It's called The David, even though that's not my name. A lot of people think it's modeled on Michelangelo's David, which is probably the idea.

The David's not number one in Europe yet, but sales are strong there too and a lot of sex blogs figure it will be by the end of the year.

The woman who makes the dildo used to be a professional dominatrix, but sales of my cock are so high that she doesn't take clients anymore. Me, I've never seen a cent from my penis. In fact, it cost me two hundred dollars.

Three years ago I went to see her. She said it was two hundred for an hour. When I showed up at her place she took the money and told me to strip. Then she tied me up. She was hot and I had a hard on. She looked at it and she smiled.

"Your cock is perfect, you know. I should take a mold of it and make a dildo," she said.

"Okay," I said.

She disappeared for ten minutes and came back with plaster, a bucket of water and a couple of pills.

"Swallow these," she said.

I did and my erection lasted two hours. "Look at that. Any longer and you're supposed to consult a physician," she said when it went down.

She put the plaster on my penis and I lay there tied up until it dried.

"It's not the length. It's not that your cock is short. Your cock is a good length. It's average I would say. It's the shape. It has a perfect arc and a nice big head. The cast takes about two hours to set, so I hope you're comfortable."

After two hours she took off the cast and then she untied me and threw me out. "Your time's up. Besides, your erection's gone down," she said.

Now thousands of women are fucking my likeness daily. Probably thousands of men too. I come in three different materials: hard plastic, silicone and polished maple.

The fact that women all over the world are fucking my likeness doesn't actually help me get laid. In fact I can't remember the last time I had sex. I've tried telling women that I'm the top selling dildo in North America, but it doesn't help, so most of the time I don't say anything.

I came close to having sex recently. I got into the woman's bedroom and we both got naked. I was on my back on her bed and she got this big smile.

"I know that cock. It's fucked me many times," she said.

It turned me right off. I went soft and I couldn't get hard again. She got really pissed off. She told me to grow up.

THE DAVID

"If you're going to be a dildo, you should expect women to use you. Christ you're pathetic. You should be honoured that I recognized you."

She reached into the top drawer of her night table and pulled out a polished maple version of my penis. She banged it on the corner of the night table.

"See. *It's* hard."

"Fuck you."

She threw the dildo at my head.

"I'm going to make sure everyone knows that their dildo has erectile dysfunction. Now get the fuck out of here," she said.

She's tried her best to ruin me as a dildo. She's posted reviews on most of the major sex blogs and online sex shops. She's printed off flyers and put them in the windows of local sex shops.

But sales keep going strong. Everyday hundreds more women are fucking my likeness and I'm celibate. I can't even enjoy masturbating anymore. All I can think about is that stupid fucking dildo. I've never had much going for me. I was never that smart or that good looking or that athletic. It turns out my only talent is to have the perfect cock and I can't even use it.

2014

The world was a better place when I was a kid. Really it was a better place anytime before 2014. That's when humanity ends.

It's all thanks to Theresa's older brother Bernie. It's kind of a bitch having the person responsible for the end of humanity as your brother-in-law.

Bernie built a machine that sent everyone throughout history back in time at the age of forty to the year they were born. He finished the machine October 28th 2014. He plugged it into the outlet above the toaster and flipped it on. It worked on the first go.

He built the machine to prove a point. When Bernie and Theresa were kids, their mom and dad talked all the time about how the world had been different when they were kids. They'd go on about candy bars that cost a nickel and how it was safe to walk the streets alone at night and how the world was quieter and people weren't as stressed. The implication was that the world had been better when they were kids.

Everybody does that, but according to Theresa her parents were really bad. Bernie hated listening to it. He thought it was self-delusion and he decided to call his parents, and all of humanity on it.

I remember talking to Bernie about it when he was building the machine.

"Why throughout history?" I said. "Why not just people today? I mean, this whole 'the world used to be a better place' is kind of a modern thing, right? I agree it's bullshit, but it's only natural. Technology is changing the world so fast."

"It's got nothing to do with technology, man. Listen, you remember Julius Caesar? Cicero was six years older than Caesar and he used to go on all the time about how Caesar and his buddies were a bunch of degenerates," Bernie said.

I shrugged and let it go. I knew Bernie was brilliant, but I thought he was more than a little crazy too and I didn't figure he could make his machine work. He did, though. I've got to admit it was a pretty good prank on humanity. As mad science goes it's up there, maybe at the top, but it's messed up a lot of lives. 1978 has seen three different US presidents since I was born and they all served out the full year.

It's amazing how much shit has stayed the same, though. Sometimes it's different people doing stuff, sometimes it's just the same people earlier. Reagan ended up serving four terms as president, the first two in the eighties, the second two in the forties.

Still, even the people who've done better on their second go around don't seem to appreciate the joke.

A few people were happy at first. Like cigarette retailers and tobacco executives. When they went back in time, suddenly the rules on advertising and where you could smoke were much looser. For them it was like going back to a golden age. It didn't last long, though. People weren't used to the smoke anymore. By 1976 anti-smoking legislations were already stricter than they had been in 2014.

2014

Humanity probably would have recovered from Bernie's joke except for a hiccup in the machine. It couldn't process anything that happened after it came online. When you get to October 28th 2014 you dead end and reset to the day you were born at whatever age you happen to be.

Bernie might have been able to fix the problem, but nobody knew about it yet when he showed up in 1972. All they knew was that his joke wasn't very funny. They lynched him thirty-two hours after he reappeared.

It wasn't until the end of 1974 that anybody could have noticed the problem, although nobody did. Theresa was the first to suspect a problem when we showed up in 1976 and we were only thirty-eight.

"What happened to 2015 and 2016?" she said.

"Fucked if I know, but wait til I get my hands on your brother," I said. Theresa was a month and a half older than me, so she already knew. "Shit, I'm sorry," I said.

Theresa had a mathematical bent. She worked on a fix for Bernie's machine until she died in 2012, but it was hard because technology had to catch back up. I thought about continuing her work, but I'm too old and I never had the aptitude for that kind of shit anyway. I passed her work on to a couple of well known physicists, but when the world looped back in 2014 all the research was lost.

It's been four years for me since Theresa died. That makes it 1978. How fucked up is that? People keep on going, but it can't last much longer. Theresa and I had two kids, one in 2011 and one in 1976. The older one's only six-and-a-half and I won't get to see him again unless I live another twenty-one years and he'll still be six-and-a-half.

That's the problem. The loop of people's lives keeps getting shorter. Eventually people will be reliving the same day over and over and over again like that movie Groundhog Day and it will seem normal to them.

I guess humanity could still save itself. Our younger one, Marcie, is talking about having kids and if she hurries, she could have one by 1979. The more time people have to work on a solution before they loop back, the better the odds of solving the problem, but personally I don't hold out much hope for humanity's salvation.

Marcie and I might both have been born in 1976, but the seventies and the eighties aren't the same as they used to be and the second generation of seventies kids are different. They lack the drive and direction that my generation had. Humanity may not end until 2014, but it's well on its way to hell.

Catsup

My best friend since childhood occasionally has really fucked up dreams. Crazy shit involving decapitations and zombie parents. Stuff a psychiatrist would have a field day with.

My dreams aren't like that. I had a dream about a ketchup bottle. It was an American bottle, because ketchup was spelled catsup. There was nobody around. Nobody poured from the bottle or anything. The dream was just about the ketchup bottle.

I told my best friend since childhood about it and he said, "Man, don't take this the wrong way, but you have the most pointless dreams."

"That's not true," I said, but it is. In thirty-five years, I've never had a dream that didn't seem pointless. I've looked for meaning in my dreams and I can't find it. Nobody else can either. It's sick. Even just one dream. Dreams are supposed to have meaning.

I went to see a psychiatrist. I told her I was there because my dreams were pointless and I needed to know why.

"No one's dreams are pointless. All dreams have meaning. It's just that sometimes that meaning is buried deep within the subconscious. Sometimes it can be hard to find the meaning, but it's there," she said.

I told her about the ketchup bottle that said catsup and she grilled me for an hour about my relationships with ketchup and with

Americans. I saw her every week for two months and then she dropped me as a patient.

"You should just learn to accept it. Be happy with who you are," she said and that was that.

I found another psychiatrist. He specialized in dream interpretations. I told him about my dreams. He thought I was making them up.

"Don't take this the wrong way, but not dreaming can be a sign of psychopathy," he said.

"I'm not making this shit up. I actually dreamt about a ketchup bottle."

He hooked me up to machines while I slept and I had dreams and he was flummoxed. After that he was obsessed with finding out what was going on in my dreams. He wanted me to see him three times a week.

"I can't afford three times a week," I said.

"Fine, I won't charge you," he said.

We did brainstorming sessions. They were mostly word association. Three times a week wasn't enough for him. He called me at work and at home in the evenings. I got fed up and told him I couldn't do it anymore. He kept calling. I had to change my number.

My best friend since childhood thought it was funny. "Shit man, maybe you should go see a psychic. They can make up a meaning for anything."

I told him to fuck off, but I went to see a psychic anyway. She advertised on Craigslist. She said she did tarot readings, palm readings, dream interpretations and for an extra fee, she'd make contact with the afterlife.

I told the psychic about my dreams and she couldn't figure them out either.

"I've gotta tell you I have no idea. But, I have a friend you should go see."

I went to see the friend. The friend was transgender, male to female. She smoked pot constantly because it helped more than the meds her doctor gave her.

"For what?" I said.

"Hmm? That's not important. We're here to figure out your dreams. You can relax. I know about dreams. In a previous life I was the Oracle at Delphi. I predicted that Alexander would conquer the world. I also predicted that Julius Caesar would become emperor of Rome," she said.

"Wasn't there a few hundred years between Alexander and Caesar?"

"I was the Oracle several lives in a row. I was so good at it that they kept renewing me."

I told her about my dreams, particularly the ketchup bottle. I had high hopes. I figured she had to be crazy enough to find meaning in my dreams. She wasn't, though. She was so disgusted by my subconscious that she threw me out after half an hour.

"See man. What have I been telling you? Look, we've known each other, what, twenty-six years?" my best friend since childhood said.

"Twenty-eight."

"Shit. Has it really been twenty-eight years? I guess so, eh. Wow. And in all that time, you've never had a dream that wasn't completely pointless."

I know my friend's right, but I don't want to believe it. I've spent hours just staring at ketchup bottles. Plastic, glass, big, small, full, empty, half-full and there's nothing. I've even tried putting the bottles in different locations around my apartment and I've gone out to restaurants and stared at their ketchup bottles.

Empirically, I can't escape it. I've suspected for a long time, but it sucks to really know. Everybody else's dreams seem to have meaning. Maybe they don't. Maybe everyone's dreams are as pointless as mine and they just lie about their dreams to feel like they're normal. Or maybe I'm just a dud.

The Nice List

They put out a list of the nicest people in the country and you didn't make it. You didn't even get an honourable mention.

Maybe if you'd put your name higher when you filled out the form. There was room for ten names. You put yourself ninth, because you didn't want it to seem too obvious.

It's a bitch because you really wanted to be on that list. It's not like you're making a list for your money or your athletic prowess. You don't even have a hope of employee of the month. You've tried, but you just can't give a shit about your job. What's amazing is that there are a couple of people at work who can.

You could try charity work and see if that helps with the next list, but that's not really niceness and besides, who has the time.

The worst part is that the Montreal Gazette got hold of all the voting in the country and published the entire survey. You've combed that survey and your name's only on it once. One person ranked you ninth.

That means that your best friend, who you've known since forever, didn't vote for you. Neither did the guy you drink with at the pub down the street who, whenever you buy him a round, tells you you're the nicest guy.

At least you won't be fooled by him again. From now on that fucker can buy his own drinks.

The Lonely

Roy Orbison is the world's greatest lover. Lothario, Don Juan, Casanova, they were amateurs. They've been nothing since they died. Not Roy Orbison. Death hasn't stopped him. He was dead for more than twenty years and still Sarah left me for him.

It started with Oh, Pretty Woman, of all the songs. Sarah'd never even heard of Roy Orbison. Her parents listened to classical music. So did Sarah. Then one day she had the radio on in the car and Oh, Pretty Woman came on.

"His voice is amazing," she said.

"Who listens to radio still?" I said.

"I was changing the CD. I can't remember the name of the guy, though. Roy or Ray or something."

I had no idea Roy Orbison was still active – he did die in 1988 – so the next day at lunch I went and bought a copy of his greatest hits. I gave it to Sarah that night. She sat perfectly still through the entire album and then we fucked. After, she got up and listened to the entire album again.

Sarah went out and bought every Roy Orbison album she could find and then she went online and ordered the ones she couldn't. She got everything, live albums, the shit from the seventies that nobody ever listened to, even The Travelling Wilburys.

"I almost like the Travelling Wilburys best. You have this anticipation of his voice. It's such a tease," she said.

Sarah was obsessed. She listened to Roy Orbison constantly. When we'd have sex, he had to be on in the background. That was weird, but I didn't say anything. Then we stopped having sex.

"You don't understand the emotion of it," she said. "It's the anticipation as much as the act itself. It's about yearning. It's supposed to be something soulful."

"It is soulful."

"No it's not."

"All right, it's not. But we've been together five years. Not every fuck can be soulful."

One afternoon I came home early and Sarah was already home. She was listening to Roy Orbison as usual. She was lying on her back with her pants undone. She was holding the album cover from Crying. She was moaning. Her body was moving forward and back and her head kept slamming into the armrest.

"Oh come on. Look at him. He was such an ugly fucker with that mop and those dark glasses."

"He was beautiful. Much better looking than you. But it doesn't matter. He was beautiful throughout. Even if he was hideous on the outside, he was so beautiful inside. Not very many people are beautiful on the inside. You aren't. You have no soul. You don't understand loneliness. You don't understand yearning," she said.

And then she left me for Roy Orbison. She packed up her clothes and her laptop and his CDs. That was all she took.

THE LONELY

It was hard. Sarah and I were together for five years. I loved her. We'd talked about getting married. Now I sit around at night and listen to music and think about what went wrong.

One night about a month after Sarah left me I was listening to Bruce Springsteen when Roy Orbison dropped by. He came in and sat on the couch beside me. It took me a second to recognize him, because he'd switched to contacts and because you could kind of see through him.

"I did a concert with him once. He has a real way with words," Roy said.

"Jesus, what the fuck are you doing here?" I said.

"Sarah went out with a friend. I wanted to come by and say sorry. I know what it's like to be lonely. You were right. I am ugly. If I wasn't a celebrity, I probably wouldn't ever have gotten laid."

"Fuck off. Get the fuck out of my house," I said.

Roy left without a fuss. Afterwards, I felt guilty and I put on one of his albums. Now he's all I listen to. It's perverse, but I can't help it. The others, they talk like they understand what it's like to be lonely, but you can tell they don't really. Roy Orbison does. I listen to his voice and it brings tears to my eyes. The way I treated him, that wasn't right.

A Melpaso Production

At one thirty in the morning I wound up on a couch in the basement with some guy. He was short and ugly, with curly dark hair and a stupid looking pencil moustache.

It was a lousy party and I was only there because my girlfriend had dumped me after two years and I'd needed to get out of the house.

"I have the best idea ever for a movie," the guy said.

"Uh-huh." The guy was drunk out of his mind.

"No, really man. It's true. The funny thing is, it'd only work as a movie. It wouldn't really work as a book or a TV show."

"Uh-huh," I said.

Then he told me his idea. It was a great idea. It couldn't miss.

"Jesus, that's not bad," I said. "Son of a bitch. That might be the best idea I've ever heard. How the fuck did you ever come up with that?"

He shrugged. "Ah man, you know. Sometimes shit just comes to you. They say everybody's got at least one story in them."

"Yeah, but I mean, Jesus. You should be careful who you tell. An idea that good, somebody'll steal it."

"I know. That's why I haven't pitched it to anybody. You're the first person I've told it to."

"Why me?" I said.

"You've got a face you can trust man," he said. He picked up a glass of gin off the coffee table, emptied it and passed out.

I thought about it. There was nobody else down there, so I bashed the guy's head in on the table. An idea like that's once in a lifetime. Not even. It was too good to pass up.

I tried to make it look like bad luck, like he'd just fallen off the couch the wrong way. It had the reek of alcohol and the whiff of plausibility.

I went upstairs and mingled for a bit. My whole body shook, but overall I managed to act pretty normal. I left around quarter after two. I didn't sleep at all.

I waited a week, because I was afraid it would look suspicious, and then I bought a ticket to LA. I tried to meet with a bunch of big producers, but they didn't know who I was, so they wouldn't see me.

After five days, I finally cornered an agent in a parking lot outside of a Denny's. It was after midnight and the lot was quiet. The guy wasn't much of a player, but he had a couple of clients that I'd heard of.

"Who the fuck are you man?" he said to me.

"I'm nobody yet, but I've got a brilliant idea for a movie. The best idea anyone's ever had. The best idea ever," I said.

"Yeah. You and everyone else."

"No. I'm serious. Trust me. You want to represent me on this."

He shrugged. "Alright. Let's hear it hotshot. Pitch it to me. But keep it brief. A hundred words or less."

I told him the idea, just like the guy on the couch had told me.

"Shit. That is a great fucking idea," the agent said. He leaned forward and put his hands on his knees and hyperventilated. "Jesus."

"So does that mean you're interested?"

"Definitely. Just hang on. Wait right here. I'll be two seconds," he said.

He walked across the parking lot. He pushed a button and a BMW started. The agent got into the BMW, backed it out and gunned it straight at me. I tried to dive out of the way, but I didn't make it. The grille crushed the left side of my skull.

The next thing I knew, I was sitting in the middle of a giant waiting room. I was on a leather couch that was in a square facing outwards. I couldn't see the ends of the room. It seemed to stretch on forever.

A woman walked by. She was about fifty, heavy set and frumpy. When she saw me, she stopped. She leaned down and took hold of my head.

"Tch. That's a nasty one," she said.

I reached up and felt my temple. There was a big divot and my hand came away sticky with blood.

"You must have just gotten here," the woman said.

"Yeah. I guess so. I'm starving. Is there somewhere around here I can get something to eat?"

"There's a vending machine right over there," she said.

I went and got a chocolate bar and a bag of chips from the vending machine and used up the last of my change. I sat back down on the couch and opened the chips. They were stale.

A guy came and sat down beside me. He was short and ugly and had dark curly hair and a pencil moustache.

"You remember me?" he said.

I looked at him carefully.

"Ho shit." That's when I figured out I was dead.

"That's right you son of a bitch. I'm the guy whose idea you stole and then you killed. You fucking beat my brains in on a coffee table. That's fucking sick. How can you live with yourself?"

"I'm dead." He threw me on the ground and my chips spilled everywhere. "That was my last buck," I said. He started kicking me. He was strong for a little guy. "Jesus. Ow, fuck, Jesus!"

"You fucking thief! You fucking thief! You stole my idea and then you fucking killed me!"

I'd killed him before I'd stolen his idea, but I decided not to quibble.

"I'm sorry," I said.

"You're sorry. Aw, he's sorry. Good for you. You're not forgiven."

He kept kicking me. I understood where he was coming from, but his kicks were sharp. I was probably bleeding internally. I wondered if I could die twice.

It went on for a while. The guy had incredible stamina. It ended when two other guys came along and pulled him off me. I caught my breath and tried to stand up, but my midsection hurt too much. I crawled as far as the couch and that was it.

"If it makes you feel any better, the guy I told your idea to ran me over with his car," I said.

He spat in my face and then he walked away.

I felt like shit for a couple of days afterwards. I mostly lay on my back on the couch. The fluorescent lights overhead made it hard to sleep, but at least I was able to eat and drink. The couch was a constant source of change for the vending machines. It was all different currencies, but the machines didn't seem to care. At one point, I pulled a handful of bronze coins with Tiberius' head on them. They were in mint condition. They would have been worth a fortune. The machine took five of them for a can of pop.

After two days of lying there, I got bored and went wandering. I decided I had to find the guy again and make it right. At least say sorry. Hopefully he wouldn't kick me this time.

While I was looking for him, I met a pretty woman who was about twenty.

"You're new here, aren't you?" she said.

I told her my story. I expected her to run away from me screaming, but she just shrugged.

"Don't feel too bad. That little shit had it coming. Nobody around here can stand him. He goes around telling everybody about this great idea as if it was his. A lot of people here had that same idea. Before he did. You'd be surprised," she said.

"I love you and I want to have sex with you. You're perfect," I said.

"Thanks. You're kind of cute, but that dent in the side of your head's not very attractive. Maybe when it heals."

We parted ways. I took to asking everybody I saw about the idea. They all seemed to know about it. Some people said it was this

Chinese guy Chen-Yu who came up with it first, and some people said it was an Iranian woman named Masoumeh. They were both killed for the idea and they both blamed the other. But the most interesting story I heard was about a South African bushman who, one day, walked out of the desert and into a casino in Johannesburg and started talking. The only person who understood what he was saying was the croupier at the roulette wheel, a white man whose family had been there since before the Boer War.

The croupier killed the bushman in the alley behind the casino. He quit his job and wrote the screenplay. He put it in an envelope and addressed it to Hollywood, but the postman was curious and he opened the envelope. He went and killed the croupier and set to retyping the screenplay with his own name on it.

That was in nineteen thirty-seven. The screenplay never got to Hollywood, because the postman burned in a suspicious fire, along with both copies of the script.

As near as I can tell, everyone who ever had the idea told it to somebody else and then got murdered. I decided that when I found that ugly little shit and his pencil moustache I'd let him have it, the lying prick. It took me three days to find him.

"I'm sorry," I said, and then he kicked the shit out of me for half an hour.

I run into him from time to time and it always goes the same way. I say I'm sorry and he kicks the shit out of me for half an hour.

It's not all bad here, though. My head is healed and the perfect twenty year old woman had sex with me. She told me there's a new guy here. I haven't run across him yet, but it sounds like the new guy is the agent who ran me over.

The rumour going around now is that Clint Eastwood's making the idea into a movie. The guy's over eighty, but nobody dares to try and kill him.

Love

This is not a story about love. Stories about love don't sell. Actually they do. They sell in supermarkets and drug stores. Who wants their stories bought in supermarkets and drug stores? The books you buy in supermarkets and drug stores are the books people get rid of when their bank has a book sale for charity. People don't want those books on their shelves in case they have someone over and that someone takes a look in the bookshelf to see what they read.

This story is about two people who are together. A man and a woman, but it doesn't have to be a man and a woman. This story's not epic, or even all that interesting, except to them.

They met on a dating website, which embarrassed them at first, but eventually it was just how they met. They only had one real date. After that she mostly lived at his place for four months and then they got a place together.

He asked her to marry him two months after they met. He was on a computer at two AM in Chile. She was in Canada. They lived in Canada. She paused for a few seconds and it felt like forever to him.

"Yes, but fuck you, you can't ask me to marry you online," she typed.

He asked her in person when he came back to Canada. They were in a hotel in Toronto. There was a pool that was too shallow and too warm and too chlorinated. He was going to ask her there, but there were other people around. When they went back up to their room, he knelt down in front of her. She had on a white hotel towel.

"Will you marry me?" he said.

"Yes," she said.

They were engaged for a while. It was life. He didn't get along with her parents, but otherwise they didn't really overcome obstacles.

They both wondered sometimes. A couple of times one of them said, "I don't know if this is going to work." The other one always said, "It will."

They got married. It was a small ceremony. Most people thought it was nice. It's tough to say how it will end up. There's time. But so far it works. It works better than most.

This is not a story about love. Stories about love wind up in the supermarket and in the drug store. These people aren't like that. I know them. This story's more about the antithesis of hate. It's modern that way. It sells better, if you don't want to sell in the supermarket and in the drug store, and people aren't ashamed to put it on their bookshelves.

Time's Person of the Year

Max and his friend Shane, who was in high school, robbed the Pronto blind. They made off with two gym bags full of chocolate bars and went and stood on the overhang by the doors for the little kids and threw the chocolate bars out for all of us.

Everybody knew where the chocolate bars came from. We all thought it was awesome, because they were free chocolate bars and because they came from the Pronto and the guy who owned the Pronto was a real asshole. All the kids would go to the Pronto after school, because there weren't any other stores around. When you went in, the guy stared at you and asked you if you were going to buy something and if you said no, he threw you out. Even if your friend was buying something.

I got six chocolate bars when Max and Shane threw them off the overhang by the doors for the little kids. I only ended up with three, because Joe didn't get any, so I had to give him two and because I gave Liz the Smarties because Liz said that Smarties were her favourite and I had a crush on Liz.

After a few minutes, Madame Martin came along and everybody on the edge of the crowd took off and everybody else tried to pretend nothing was going on. Madame Martin knew what was going on, but she played dumb. She said school was out and it was time to go home and then she walked to her car.

The next morning Max got called down to the principal's office anyway, and he said the cops went by the high school where Shane went and arrested him. Max said the old fucker at the Pronto didn't have a clue who'd done it, because they were really smart about it, and somebody must've told.

Somebody was Billy. Billy was the biggest tattletale in the whole school, and he'd been at the back of the crowd, so he didn't get any chocolate bars and when he asked around, nobody'd give him one, because nobody liked him anyway.

Max got suspended for a week over the whole thing, and his parents and Shane's parents had to pay back the old fucker who owned the Pronto to get him to drop the charges against them. Billy got the shit kicked out of him, over and over. Most of the guys in grade seven and eight took a turn. Sara too, because she was five-ten and could take anybody in the school except Max and Jared.

I didn't get to beat up Billy. The whole school wanted to, so we agreed to go alphabetically. We got as far as the Rs and my last name's Tanner. When we were on the Rs Billy started going to the vice-principal's office after school. He waited there until his parents came and picked him up, everyday for two months until school ended for the summer. The next year, Billy went to a different school.

Now Time has named Billy the person of the year. He made a mint on a couple of start ups and he's donating all his time and money to development in Africa. Max is doing three years for assault.

TIME'S PERSON OF THE YEAR

It's good what Billy's doing now, but when I look back on it, I still wish my name had been Fitzgerald or Jenkins or something.

Jaczek

I lasted over a year on the night shift, which was longer than most guys. Most guys lasted about a month. It was shit work. We cleaned industrial spaces between ten pm and six am.

There were twelve of us at any one time. Mostly we worked in crews of two or three for the night. We were all bottom feeders. You have to be a bottom feeder to apply for work like that. A lot of the guys were ex-cons. It was all guys while I was there.

We got minimum wage, there weren't any benefits, and the boss was a dick. He was fifty years old and fifty pounds overweight and he had a thick brown moustache. He coached his son's minor hockey team and he wore the jacket everywhere. Whenever he saw me he'd ask if I had a girlfriend, and then he'd tell me some story about the twenty-five year old woman he was fucking that week.

It must've been partly true about the women, because sometimes he'd bring one around the office or on an inspection. They were always young and beautiful. A week after I started, he showed up with a woman who couldn't have been more than twenty.

"What the hell does she see in that fat fuck?" I said to Gus. Gus had been with the company for six months. That made him third in seniority.

"Money, man. It's all about money college boy. You might be educated but you're broke, same like the rest of us," Gus said.

Everybody there called me college boy, except for Jaczek.

"Where do you get college boy from? I dropped out after my first year," I said.

"But you went. And you make sure everyone knows that you went."

"So?"

"So you act like you're all better than the rest of us. Look at you. You don't smoke and you don't drink and you dress good and you talk good."

"Well," I said.

"See what I mean, college boy?"

Jaczek had been there longer than anybody. Somebody said he'd been there seven years, but I never asked him. Jaczek was sixty. He'd come over from Poland in ninety-three. He was mostly a communist and he was entirely an alcoholic.

The other guys didn't like working with Jaczek, because he was always drunk and he was always drinking, but he didn't share. My first night on the job, I got put with him.

"He's okay. Just don't let him drive the van. You let him drive the van and you're fired," the boss said.

It was just the two of us. We had to clean a kitchen that supplied a chain of local coffee shops. We just had to do the stuff that was out of reach of the cooking staff. It was an industrial design, with the rafters and the ducting visible. We had two air compressors attached to hoses to blast the dirt off.

We covered everything on the floor in plastic before we started.

"You know, most of these places, they can't tell what you do," Jaczek said. He took a flask out of his coat. He took a swig of whatever it was and put the flask back without offering me anything. Then he sat down.

"What are you doing?" I said.

"I watch. Make sure you're not gonna fall off. I go up those ladders, I kill myself." He took another nip from his flask.

I put up a ladder and plugged in one of the air compressors. I worked my ass off. Jaczek sat. After an hour he got up and turned on a radio that was sitting on one of the counters.

"You have terrible radio in this country," he said. He flipped through a few stations and settled on radio two. It was playing a symphony, but I don't know classical music.

"Are you going to help at all?" I said.

"Music helps. It's not good to do this kind of work without music."

He took out a pen and some paper and wrote. I don't know what he wrote. Around three, he put the pen and paper down and fell asleep. He snored.

At five, the kitchen staff came in. I kicked Jaczek awake. He wiped his eyes and snorted and took a hit from his flask.

"The place is all yours," I said to the staff. I put the ladder away and cleared out the plastic and we left.

Most nights I ended up with Jaczek and he never did any work. He sat and drank and listened to music and slept. Sometimes he wrote.

One night he looked at me and said, "What do you work so hard for?"

"I wouldn't work so hard if you'd do something," I said.

"You don't have to work so much. These companies, they do not know. If they really cared, they would do the work themselves. They would not hire us."

I ignored Jaczek and went back to work. I did my best, but I hated the job. After two months, I tested Jaczek's theory. We were working in a warehouse off St Laurent Boulevard. I worked for ninety minutes and decided I'd had enough. I sat down and listened to music and watched Jaczek write. After a bit, he closed his book. He took a nip from his flask and fell asleep.

I sat for another half hour, then I got up and went over to Jaczek. I took his flask from his coat pocket and had a belt. It was straight vodka. I nearly gagged. I was curious about what he wrote, so I opened his book, but it was all in Polish and I couldn't make out a word.

I drank the rest of the vodka. Normally I didn't drink so the alcohol hit me hard. Around four I ran to the toilet and threw up. I was still drunk at the end of our shift and Jaczek had to drive the van.

The boss was at the depot when we got back. That was pretty unusual. He looked at Jaczek and he pulled me aside.

"Why the fuck was he driving?" the boss said.

"He really wanted to," I said.

"I told you never to let him drive. What the fuck, college boy?"

"I don't know. He seems okay. He slept for a bit. I think he slept it off."

"Jesus. You're fucking drunk," the boss said. "You god damned fucking idiot. Get the fuck out of here. And if you come in drunk again, you're fucking fired."

The next night I got put with two different guys. One of them had started around the same time as me. The other guy, it was his second night.

"Hey college boy. I heard you drank Jack's vodka," the first guy said.

"Isn't it Jaczek?"

"This is Canada man. It's Jack here. So is it true?"

"Yeah, it's true."

I slacked off at work. Only the new guys ever did any work. They were suckers. Once in a while a company complained to the boss about our work and one or two people got fired, but mostly nobody noticed.

In the next eleven months, I didn't work with Jaczek again. Sometimes I saw him at the start or end of a shift. I'd say "hey" and he'd say "hey" and that was it, but I don't think he held a grudge over the vodka.

For Christmas I got him a twenty-six ounce bottle of vodka to apologize for drinking his. I didn't get anything for anybody else at work. Not even the boss.

The last night I worked the job I was with Matt. Matt had been there four months, which was longer than most. The boss came by at midnight. He was with a woman half his age. She stared at me the whole time, until the boss went to the bathroom. I took her aside.

"What are you doing with that asshole?" I said.

"Who should I be with?" she said.

"Me."

"You?"

"Hey, I'm not going to be doing this forever. I'm going to university during the day," I lied.

"Really?"

"Really. I only need three more credits to graduate. I'll be done in the spring."

"You're kinda cute too," she said.

"I want you."

"Give me half an hour to lose Stanley. I'll meet you back here."

She left with the boss, but she came back an hour later. We went into the bathroom and locked the door. We were in there a long time.

The next morning Matt told everyone.

"He told her he was going to university and she fell for it. She thinks he's going to be somebody," Matt said.

"So?" Jaczek said.

"What's your problem old man?" Matt said.

"So shut the fuck up about it. It's not your business," Jaczek said.

"Fuck you, you alcoholic old Polack shit for brains. Besides, it's the boss's business. I bet he'd like to know what the college boy's been doing."

"You tell the boss and I kill you. Anyone tells the boss and I kill them," Jaczek said.

Somebody told the boss. That night I showed up for work and the boss was standing there with his arms crossed.

"You're fired," he said.

"You've gotta give me two weeks' notice," I said.

"Get the fuck out of here."

"Sure, but you still owe me."

He leaned in close to me. He stank of cigarettes and coffee. "I know that you fucked that little cunt whore. Now get out of here you little asshole. And if I see you again I'm gonna kill you."

I left. The boss ripped me off. He didn't pay me my two weeks of severance. He didn't even pay me for the last week and a half that I worked. I should've sued, but I didn't.

I don't know if it was Matt who told the boss, but two weeks after I got fired, Matt fell off a ladder. He had an air-compressor hose with him. It wrapped around his throat and strangled him on the way down. His head split open when it hit the floor too.

I doubt Jaczek had anything to do with it, but every Christmas I send him a twenty-six ounce bottle of vodka just in case.

The Dream Tax

The consensus was that the government and politics generally were out of ideas. Even the politicians noticed. In the last election the Prime Minister fell asleep in the middle of one of the leaders' debates. He won anyway. People said they voted for him because at least falling asleep was honest.

After the election, the government set up a commission to study the problem and they came back with a dream tax. Nothing major, just one seventh they said. One seventh of the nation's dreams could provide a lot of fresh ideas they said.

Now everyone over the age of eighteen has to hook themselves up to a machine one night a week and that night's dreams belong to the government.

The tax passed easily enough. Only four MPs voted against it. The people weren't such big fans. A bunch of pop icons got together and said, "You can't put a tax on people's dreams." They wrote a song and a play and toured with it. I saw it when it came to the National Arts Centre.

The show wasn't any hell, but that's not the point. The point is the pop icons were wrong. You can put a tax on people's dreams. It's done. There were administrative headaches at first as they tried to make the machines available to the public, and despite a recent decline there are still a number of people dodging the tax, but it's no more than the number of people dodging income taxes.

I dodged the tax at first, but dream tax dodging has been shown to lead to sleep disorders. Dodging the tax involves forcing yourself to stay awake through the eight hour period you're hooked up. The thing is the eight hour period is carefully set to coincide with your normal sleep cycle. The dodgers drink caffeine and pop pills to stay awake. You can pick out the long-term dodgers right away, because they can't sleep anymore. They wander around day and night like zombies.

I dodged for six months and then had to do a year of sleep therapy to get back to normal.

The dream tax is a pilot project. The government built in a five year sunset clause in case of unforeseen consequences. The five years is up this May.

Most people you ask say they want the tax gone, but expert opinion is mixed. They say there's no evidence the project has succeeded in its aims, but it has put Canada at the forefront of dream capture technology and that's worth something.

Especially now that the US, Europe and China are all considering a similar system to the one here. It would look bad if Canada eliminated the tax at the same time as other nations instituted it.

The Prime Minister has been stumping for the tax lately. "We have passed several pieces of important legislation based on the dreams we have received, that the Canadian people have so generously donated. Canadians have always had that spirit of self-sacrifice and a desire to make society better," he said in a TV commercial and you know he's serious because the commercial's getting lots of air time.

It doesn't seem to matter that none of the new legislation makes sense, like the law that forbids turning your back to put on a mask and the one that makes it illegal to throw fruit to someone for the purpose of eating it.

My younger sister and her friend have started picketing on Parliament Hill for the repeal of the tax. They get good crowds, but most of the picketers are tax-dodging zombies or sixteen and seventeen year olds who aren't subject to the tax yet.

Still, people are generally against the tax and the government is said to be considering dream credits, so that at the end of the year people who dream more will get a return.

My sister says that's not enough. Her and her friend go to Parliament Hill every day. She keeps bugging me to join her. I keep saying maybe, but I never go. I'm against the tax, but I just don't dream about rebellion and social change the way I used to.

2.1

I grew up with this guy S. Actually it was only half an S. The half an S was short for Scott.

S was point one of a person. Literally. He was one hand, two eyes, an ear canal, three toes, a knee joint, a tongue and a testicle. That was all there was of him. It took some getting used to. He looked like a play-dough sculpture gone wrong.

S sat right in front of me in grade one. He had to sit on the desk to see anything and the teacher didn't like that. Nobody wanted S around. Even the parents would say stuff and point at him when they came to pick up their kids.

On the first day of grade three, the new girl, Katie, finally noticed S at two o'clock in the afternoon. When she saw him she screamed, threw her math book at him and ran to the back of the classroom to get away. Katie turned out to be a dead shot. She got S right between the eyes and he fell backwards off his desk. S didn't say anything. The teacher either.

The only person who ever paid any attention to S was his older sister Laura who walked home with him. Laura was two years older than us. She was totally normal.

I became friends with S because I felt sorry for him, but it turned out that he was pretty cool.

S also had an older brother and the older brother was normal too. So were his parents. His father was five foot ten and his mother was five foot four and they had all their body parts, and they went about their business like S wasn't there. They got him all the coolest toys though.

S was fun to hang out with. We'd go to corner stores and play arcade games. S was good. He usually had the high score on whatever game we played. He only had the one hand, but he could move from the joystick to the buttons and back with unbelievable speed. On the way out of the stores S would take a couple of chocolate bars for us while I distracted the guy at the cash. We always got away with it, because S was so small that nobody noticed him.

He was smart too. He knew a lot about a lot of stuff. He didn't do well in school, because he didn't try. He said the teachers hated him and they felt more justified hating him if he did badly.

S and I also went to high school together. His parents wanted to send him to a different school, one where people didn't know him they said, but S wouldn't let them, which was good. S was a great friend to have in high school. He was smooth. He had good taste in music and clothes and somehow he seemed to know about girls. Girls didn't like him, but he helped them like me.

The girl I really wanted was Laura, but she was two years older than me. S might have helped me out with her too, but I didn't have the guts to tell him I liked his sister.

One day in grade eleven I was in physics, first period after lunch. S was my lab partner and he wasn't there and the teacher had this horrible monotone so I put my head down and fell asleep. Halfway through the period Mrs Hendrick the vice-principal came in.

"Class, I'm afraid I have some bad news. S is no longer with us," she said.

Nobody else in the class gave a shit and I could tell by looking at Mrs Hendrick that she didn't either, but it made me sad.

Everybody in grade eleven got a morning off school to go to the funeral. Most of us went because it was a morning off school.

S' older brother Mike was there. He was in university now. He looked like a younger, thinner version of his dad. Laura was there too. Laura was different from before. I'd had a crush on her for four years. I'd memorized every contour of her body and all of her movements. From across the room I could tell that something wasn't right. She dragged her left leg when she walked and that was new, but there was more than just that.

Up close I could see her left eye and ear were missing and so was most of her right arm. I felt a lump in my throat. I stayed away from her, because I couldn't face it. She'd been so beautiful.

The funeral was weird. Nobody talked about what had happened to S, or to Laura. The priest gave the eulogy and nobody from S' family spoke.

As soon as the priest was done I ducked outside. Derek from Mr Peters' English Class was leaning against the wall of the chapel smoking a cigarette. He gave me one and I smoked it. I bought a pack that afternoon from the guy who ran the smoke shop by the school and I smoked for four months.

My mom bugged me for four months about how smoking stunts your growth. I was five-ten when I started smoking and I'm still five-ten, so maybe she was right.

I finished high school and knocked around from one job to the next. I went out with a few girls, but Laura was always in the back of my thoughts and I wasn't very good at dating without S to give me advice.

After three years of that I went to university. University was mostly drinking and muddling through. At the start of my third year, I ran into Laura at a bar. She still had the limp and she was still missing most of her right arm, but she'd gotten a glass eye and she wore her hair long and pulled over to the left side so you couldn't tell so much about the ear. She was still beautiful.

She saw me and she recognized me. She kind of nodded and then turned away. I went after her. I caught up to her at the bar and put my hand on her left arm. She started and then smiled slightly. The bar was crowded and loud and I couldn't hear shit, but somehow I convinced Laura to go with me to the coffee shop across the street.

I got black coffee and she got blueberry tea. She smiled at me, but her face was sad. That was new too since the accident.

"You know you were S' only friend," she said.

"What happened?"

"It's complicated."

"Usually when a person dies, people talk about it. They rail about the tragedy of it, shit like that," I said.

"S wasn't a person."

"Laura …"

2.1

"There was a mix up when my parents got married. The census data they had said that the average couple has two point one kids, but it turned out the information was out of date. The new data had been collected, but it hadn't been published yet. It took them more than sixteen years to figure it out."

"What?"

"Don't be normal. You can't be whole if you're normal I don't think," Laura said and then she got up and walked out.

I thought a lot about what Laura said, but I couldn't help it. I was sick of school so I dropped out and got a job. Eventually I called Laura's parents and they gave me her number. I called Laura and asked her out and she said no. I kept calling her until she finally said okay. We went for dinner and then we walked along the beach by the river. Her right leg gave her a lot of trouble so we sat down in the sand. She was so beautiful, but so sad. She was different from S. She let it bother her. I didn't care. I loved her anyway. I went to kiss her, but she pulled back.

"I wasn't kidding about being normal," she said.

I told her it didn't matter. I told her I wasn't whole anyway. I told her I'd loved her since I was twelve. I told her she was different but in a good way and I asked her to marry me. She told me I didn't understand what that meant and I told her I did, but Laura was right. I love her, but if I'd truly understood I would have left her sitting on the beach.

Thirtysomething

When I turned thirty my girlfriend, Marcie, insisted on a big party. She invited my parents and my sisters and my friends. She even invited Gerry who was only my friend on Facebook. I hadn't seen Gerry in twelve years.

I told her I didn't want a big party. "You only turn thirty once," she said and we had the party.

At the party people slapped me on the back and shook my hand and shit. The people under thirty said I was old and the people over thirty said I was respectable.

Gerry showed up. He was two months younger than me. He came up to me and shook my hand and then he slapped me on the back. "Congratulations old man," he said.

"You came," I said.

"Hey, you only turn thirty once buddy."

I played along. I even figured they were right, but they weren't. I turned thirty the next year too. It wasn't like my father who pretended he was turning twenty-nine every year. I actually turned thirty again.

All my ID said I was turning thirty again, but I didn't change it. And somehow everyone knew I was turning thirty again. Even me. My older sister, Deirdre, was the only one. "Didn't you turn thirty last year?" she said, but nobody else thought so and she shrugged and said, "Sometimes I forget how young you are."

Marcie insisted on a big party. "You only turn thirty once," she said.

I started to question that. My best friend was already thirty-two, but he was only a year older than me and Marcie was going to be twenty-nine, but she was two years younger than me. It didn't add up.

I thought about it for a while and I decided that turning thirty the first time hadn't happened. The party, everything was a dream, so I did it again. Marcie invited this guy Gerry who was only my friend on Facebook. I hadn't seen Gerry in twelve years. We wound up talking and I asked him how long it had been.

"Exactly a year is my guess. You were supposed to call me for coffee, remember?" Gerry said.

"What do you mean?"

"The big party you had last year when you turned twenty-nine. By the way, congratulations on turning thirty. Finally respectable after all these years."

Gerry was already thirty. According to his drivers' license he was ten months older than me, but my birthday was in April and we were in the same class from grade one and I hadn't skipped a grade.

"Did you start school a year late, Gerry?" I said.

"No, why?"

"No, no reason. I don't know what I was thinking."

I went along with it all because I knew turning thirty twice sounded insane, but then I turned thirty again the next year. And the year after that. My friends and family started to look at me funny, but they never questioned that I was turning thirty. It was like they knew something wasn't right, but they couldn't quite figure out what it was.

I was the same way. My memory didn't seem to get longer. I didn't feel older and when I went back over what had happened the year before and the year before and so on, it seemed like it was right that I was turning thirty.

When Marcie and I were both thirty, we got married. At that point I still wasn't sure that I was turning thirty over and over. When Marcie was thirty-eight, we split up. That made eight years we'd been married. She said that I was only twenty-two when we got married, but I remembered being older than her.

After we split up, I went to my doctor and told him how I was turning thirty over and over and he laughed. My doctor was seventy and still practising.

"Some people have trouble with thirty," he said. "Trust me, you were twenty-nine last year."

"Can you even still tell at your age?" I said and he referred me to a psychiatrist.

The psychiatrist heard my story and told me I was nuts, but he couldn't succeed in diagnosing me as anything. It seemed to piss him off. He prescribed a few different medications. They fucked up my sleep schedule and made me cranky and I quit my job because I couldn't function, but the medications didn't help with the feeling that I had been thirty for a long time.

When my little sister turned thirty-seven, I pointed out to my mother that she was my younger sister.

"Don't be silly," my mom said. "She's not your younger sister. She's seven years older than you. We call her your little sister because she's so much smaller than you."

"She's bigger than Deirdre, and I was older than her growing up," I said.

"No, no," my mom said, but she looked unsure. "Well she is bigger than Deirdre."

My doctor mentioned something about me to a colleague. The colleague had a crazy geneticist friend that he said something to and the crazy geneticist friend called me.

"Look, you're probably out of your mind, but you may as well come in for testing and we can make sure," he said.

I went to see the guy. He took samples of everything: hair, skin, blood, saliva, urine, faeces. He even took a smear from inside my mouth. After that, I went back to my life. Every now and then, he called me up and I went in to his lab and gave him more samples.

About a year after I first went to see him, the crazy geneticist called me up and told me to come in. I showed up and his two daughters were sitting there. His daughters were eighteen and twenty-three and they were both hot as hell.

"I want you to inseminate them," he said and they didn't blink.

"What?" I said.

"You were right. You really are turning thirty over and over again. It's fascinating. And the best part is there doesn't seem to be any way to tell. I can't figure out how many times you've already turned thirty, although I would like to run some more tests if you're okay with that."

"I think I'd rather be crazy," I said.

"No, no. Don't you see? It's perfect. You don't seem that dim to me. You have a huge genetic advantage. Even my eighteen year old here says you're attractive. I've shown her pictures. Does he not live up to the pictures? But older people think of you as an adult and they take you seriously. And the gene is dominant and not recessive, which means you have a good chance of passing it on. You are the father of the future."

I wasn't sure about being the father of the future, but I fucked both of his daughters and that was something. I got the younger one pregnant right away. It was seven months before the older one got pregnant.

My relationship with the daughters was weird. We were friendly and we had sex regularly, but it was like a business relationship.

The younger sister had a boy and the crazy geneticist tested him and he had the gene. Then the older sister had a boy and he had the gene too. A year after that, the younger sister had a girl and she had the gene. I was three for three at passing it along.

The crazy geneticist published all of this in the journal Science. It got picked up by National Geographic and then by the newspapers. Little stories about me popped up all over the world.

A lot of people claimed the whole thing was a hoax. My birth certificate kept changing on its own? How could that be genetic?

Some people believed though. Women stalked me. They called me up and emailed me and showed up at my door. I got rid of my Facebook profile, but it didn't help. I became like a stud dog. Mostly, the women rented hotel rooms and I showed up and fucked them. It was fun at first, but it became a drag. Not all the women I had sex with were hot and even the ones who were couldn't hold my interest.

I got into fetishes. Whips and cages and chains, shit like that. I made them force me to fuck them. That worked for a while, but then it got boring too.

I became depressed and couldn't get it up at all. That wasn't a relief. People wrote about it. They wanted to know when I'd get my hard on back. Viagra and Cialis both offered me free pills if I'd do commercials for them. I turned them down. Other companies came along with clinical trials. They shoved them into my mailbox and between my doors. They always came with a long list of everything they could accomplish and how taking them could change my life. I threw the trials in the garbage.

I started to think about my own mortality. If I stayed thirty forever, would I die of natural causes? If so, was my life expectancy the same as other people's? How many goddamned times had I already turned thirty, anyway?

When I read through reports and when I remembered what had happened, it was like I hadn't been thirty. My oldest son was six and it seemed like I was twenty-four when he was born. My ex-wife was close to fifty. It seemed like a lifetime ago. I'd been young and I'd sought out a mother figure.

That's how the newspapers remembered it too, when they wrote about me. People wrote more and more about how could it be if I'd only been "twenty-six when." The geneticist really was fucking crazy. So was I.

THIRTYSOMETHING

It's estimated that I have over a thousand kids now. Think what that means. Mostly the kids are born one at a time and most of the women I fucked didn't get pregnant the first go.

I can't do this anymore. It drives you insane. If the geneticist isn't crazy then he's at least wrong. The mutation's meant to die out. Now it might be too late for that, but at least I can stop. My offspring are all still kids and there's time for shit to happen to them. It's horrible to think about your kids that way, but I don't even know most of them.

Maybe there won't be enough of them to catch on. Maybe I can at least make them aware and they'll decide to let the mutation die out. It's not likely with over a thousand kids, though.

Either way, I'm done with it. They say under the chin is the surest way to do it. If I miss, by the time they find me, the car will be full of carbon monoxide.

"I Love You"

When Davey was a kid his mom's favourite song was that song by Jim Croce that goes, "I'll have to say I love you in a song." Davey thought that was how it should be. He determined never to just say the words, "I love you."

It was better to sing a thing like that, even if your voice wasn't any good. Singing words took an honesty that saying them didn't. For example it was easy to say, "I didn't eat the last cookie," even if you did.

Davey thought that "I love you," was sacred. That's why he was thirty-one and he had never told anyone other than his mother that he loved them.

Davey had had lovers. He was good-looking and he was likeable and he wasn't shy. Women had told Davey that they loved him. Several times. Davey figured that not saying, "I love you," back had cost him four and a half relationships. Half a relationship because he'd wanted that one to end.

Twelve days before his thirty-second birthday Davey saw a woman walking down Richmond Road and fell instantly in love with her. She had tight blonde curls and glasses and the curls bounced when she walked.

Davey stopped in the street overwhelmed. He watched her walk by and couldn't make himself move or say anything and she got away.

Twelve days before his thirty-second birthday Davey lived with Andrea. Andrea had said, "I love you," to Davey and she kept bugging him to say it back. Davey did his best to stall. Now he was ready to sing the words, "I love you," just not to Andrea.

Davey went back to that same spot on Richmond Road the next day at the same time, but his love wasn't there. He went back again the next day and the next and the next and so on. He saw her again the day before his thirty-second birthday.

This time Davey didn't freeze. He flashed her a smile and asked her if she had time for a coffee. "I'll buy. The coffee shop's right there," he said.

"I suppose I could have time for a coffee," she said.

They sat and talked and drank coffee and then they walked down to the river and talked. She liked Davey. Otherwise she wouldn't have gone to the river with him. She was mostly single. She had an old boyfriend from high school who she called sometimes when she was bored, but she didn't mention him, because she liked Davey. She wasn't sure about meeting a guy off the street, but she'd met guys off the internet, and that wasn't much different.

Then Davey got down on one knee and sang, "I love you," from Hello by Lionel Ritchie and she said, "What?"

Davey sang, "I'm in love with you," from Tramp by Otis Redding.

"I LOVE YOU"

She laughed. "I'm serious," Davey said. "Every time I tried to tell you, the words just came out wrong, so I'll have to say I love you in a song."

She started to walk away. "But I love you still," Davey sang from Build Me Up Buttercup by the Foundations.

"Okay, this is getting creepy," she said and then she was gone. Davey had no idea how she disappeared so quickly.

He stood by the river without her and he felt a lump come up in his throat. The only woman he'd ever loved had laughed at him. He blinked tears away and walked home. It was nice out, warm and sunny with just a hint of a breeze.

Davey got home right at sunset. Andrea came into the foyer while Davey was taking off his shoes.

"I can't do this anymore," she said. "How can I? I need you to say I love you, or it's over," she said.

Davey looked at her and at his shoes, and felt the lump in his throat.

"I love you," he said.

Adrian

Adrian asked me to marry him. We'd been together almost two years, but it still seemed soon.

"I need some time to think about it," I said. I could see he took that answer hard.

I loved Adrian, but he was weird about sex. He insisted on fucking me from behind while I was in the foetal position. That part was okay, but I had to be hugging Manny my childhood teddy bear while he fucked me.

The only other guy who'd fucked me on the side like that was this guy when I was fifteen. We fucked in my bedroom and Manny was on the bed then too, watching me, but I didn't hold him.

The guy was twenty. He worked for the company that was redoing the roof. He was the gopher. He kept his hand over my mouth the whole time because he didn't want me to scream. It was hard to breathe like that.

"Sometimes it can sneak up on you and then you just scream. Especially the first time," he said. "And if we get caught, we're both fucked."

I bit his hand and he pulled it away. "My parents aren't home," I said.

"The guys are on the roof," he said and he put his hand back.

Somebody must've figured out that we'd been fucking, because the roofers didn't show up the next day. They didn't show up the day after that, either. My dad called them, but they wouldn't pick up and they wouldn't call him back. My parents didn't even pay for the shingles.

I never told my parents what happened. The only person I ever told was Maggie. I didn't even tell Adrian. When Adrian asked me to marry him, I told Maggie about Adrian too.

"Man that's just fucked up. You should end it with him," Maggie said.

"That seems extreme," I said.

"God, he's probably got a thing for little girls. What if you have kids? Could you imagine him holding your little girl while she slept with her favourite stuffed animal?"

I wasn't sure I wanted to end it, but it ended anyway. Mostly thanks to Maggie. She called the cops and told them she was pretty sure that Adrian liked little girls.

The cops got warrants for Adrian's computer at work and his laptop at home. They found a couple of pages in his history with underage models. The models weren't naked. Mostly they were in tight jeans or in pyjamas.

Adrian figured I'd called the cops, but he never said it. His friend Graham did. Graham called me one night at two in the morning.

"You cunt fucking whore! He asked you to marry him," Graham said and then he hung up. He sounded drunk.

A month after the cops seized Adrian's computers, Adrian stepped in front of a bus. The bus didn't even slow up. It was downtown and there were a lot of people around. They all said it looked like Adrian wasn't paying attention. I didn't go to the funeral, but I cried when I heard. When Adrian asked me to marry him, I'd thought about saying yes.

I have a new boyfriend now, though. My new boyfriend likes to fuck with me on top. Sometimes I think about Adrian and I miss him. Even still, when I fuck my new boyfriend, I always push Manny onto the floor.

Assertiveness Training

When I was ten we got a dog. My sisters and me bugged our parents for years before they gave in and got us Milo.

My dad knew about dogs. "You have to be assertive with them," he said.

My dad was good at being assertive with Milo. If Milo wouldn't sit, he'd push him down. My dad yanked the leash to get Milo to do almost everything.

Milo was just a puppy, so he was always biting and I was scared of him.

"You have to be firm with him," my dad said and then he whacked Milo on the nose. "Look, it's not like a kid. Dogs are tough. They're used to that kind of thing. It's how they learn." Then he cuffed Milo and knocked him onto his back.

Milo learned quickly. He listened well to everybody, but he especially listened to my dad. My dad taught me to be assertive and after awhile Milo obeyed me almost as well as he obeyed my dad.

I was good at being assertive, but I always felt guilty about it. I'd take Milo for walks and people would always stop and pet him and say how well behaved he was. They never said hi to me, just to Milo. I felt like they knew my secret: that a dog that obedient had to have an assertive owner.

When I was thirteen, I let Milo go. We were in the woods. I told him to sit and stay and then I walked away. Halfway home I started crying. I cried so hard I threw up, and after I went back for him. He was sitting in the same spot waiting for me.

Milo was a good dog. Sometimes I think about him and I miss him. The only thing is, I wish he'd been disobedient. At least a little bit. I wish my father had been wrong.

My daughter's eleven and she wants a dog. Her mom thinks it's a good idea.

"It'll teach her responsibility and it'll teach her how to be assertive. She's too passive, that one," her mom said.

"I don't know. Dogs are a lot of work."

"Yeah, but they're nice too. You talk all the time about Milo. Don't you want your daughter to have those kinds of memories?"

The truth is I don't. My wife's never owned a dog so she doesn't understand, and it'll be like it was with my dad. I'll be assertive with the dog and I'll show our daughter how to be assertive.

I don't want that. I don't want her to know how to be assertive, and I don't want her to know that I know how to be assertive.

The Monster Under the Bed

Two years ago I went out with Marcie. Marcie had a son named Joey. Marcie and I were pretty serious and I spent four or five nights a week at her place. Joey was six then. Every night when Marcie put Joey to bed, Joey went on about monsters. He was obsessed with monsters. He had to have the light on in his room. Marcie couldn't even turn it off in the middle of the night because if Joey woke up and had to pee he'd scream.

One night when she went out I agreed to watch Joey. At bedtime I flipped the light off and he howled. He said the monster would get him now.

"Which monster is that?" I said.

"The one under the bed."

"There's no monster under the bed."

"Yes there is."

I turned the light on. "There's no monster under the bed. I'll prove it." I got down on my knees and looked under the bed. It was a fucking mess under there. Chocolate bar wrappers, chip crumbs, empty beer bottles, skin magazines, even an old stogie. In the middle of it all there was a monster.

It had hollowed out a spot in the floor so it could sit upright. It was looking right at me. Its eyes got big and it tried to make a break for it, but it wasn't very fast. I grabbed its arm and dragged it out from under the bed.

It bit my hand and then turned and snarled at Joey and I slapped it around a bit. It was a pretty big monster, I guess. It was only about four feet tall, but it must have been two hundred pounds. It had a big pot belly and thick grey fur full of potato chip crumbs. It tried to fight back against me at first, but it wasn't in any kind of shape and after a minute it just tried to cover itself up.

I grabbed the monster by the ear and dragged it outside and told it I'd better never see it again. Then I went inside and cleaned up under the bed. I left the light on in Joey's room, but he didn't sleep.

"Thanks for getting rid of the monster, but you didn't need to be so mean to him," he said and I went into the living room to watch TV.

Marcie came home and Joey told her all about what happened. She didn't believe him and I didn't back him up, but still, things weren't the same between us after that. Two weeks later she broke up with me. "Joey's scared of you, you know. He's convinced you're mean," she said.

I went downtown to a bar and had a couple of drinks. When I came out the monster was standing on the corner with a cardboard sign that said, "every little bit helps." He had an empty coffee cup in front of him and I chucked a quarter in on the way by.

"Thanks. A quarter. That really makes up for costing me my job," he said. "No place to go, no place to stay and nobody'll hire me now. Not even the fucking fly-by-night sweatshops that have started springing up everywhere."

I got in a cab and the monster got in beside me.

"I used to be one of the best, you know. I had a lot of seniority, my pick of locations and hours and a good pension. Then it turned out that they'd run the pension fund into the ground and they laid me off because I was making too much. I mean I lost a lot of money over the years gambling and drinking and whoring, don't get me wrong.

"Six months later, I get hired back on, but I'm on contract, two nights a week harassing your girlfriend's kid. The pay's half what I was making twenty years ago and there's no benefits. My teeth hurt like hell all the time. The dentist says that I have abscesses in two different teeth, but I can't afford to do anything about them.

"I'm not young, you know. My dad, he was dead by my age, but here I am still working. Or I was. Once upon a time the union would've gone to bat for me, but all these sweatshops have broken the unions and I'm only a contract worker so I'm not worth the fight."

I let the monster get out of the car with me and I let him come in. We sat up late and watched Ghostbusters and ate popcorn. Except for the self-pity he turned out to be a pretty cool monster. Spanish was his first language, but he'd picked up English when he was assigned to a British ex-pat's kid in Costa Del Sol.

"Spain's beautiful, man. Canadians all think they live in this gorgeous wilderness paradise, but I'd pick just about anywhere over this shit, no offence. But you've got to go where the jobs are."

"Listen, can I ask you something? Do you think I'm mean?" I said.

"No more so than anybody else."

"Marcie broke up with me because Joey thought I was too mean to you. Was I too mean to you?"

"I don't know man. I probably would've slapped me around too. The ear might have been a little much. At that point I was going, but it's pretty natural I think. Don't beat yourself up over it."

I let the monster stay for three weeks. We'd hang out in the evenings and drink and watch movies. He was really into European porn for some reason. "Especially the Germans. There's something about that accent. I love when the German women are bossing the men around. That's hot."

"You're not into monsters?"

"Where am I going to find monster porn? It's not like there's an underground monster corner store I can pop into."

I liked hanging out with him. It was like being twenty again, but he didn't do anything except eat, drink, talk and sleep. I told him he should go get a job, but he kept saying nobody would hire him after what happened.

"What about a desk job somewhere? Somebody must coordinate kids' beds."

"Sure, but I'm a field monster. For forty years. I can't be a clerk pushing paperwork."

I tried to help him do up a resume, but he'd sabotage it while I was at work and I'd have to start over.

After three weeks of that I kicked him out. "You know how it'll end up," he said. "I thought maybe I'd be different. It was changing for a while, but I guess it'll be the same for me as it was for my dad. All his generation really. I'll end up face down in a ditch and your dogs'll chew on me and you'll wonder what it is they're always getting into in that one spot."

I gave him two hundred bucks when I threw him out. He probably spent it on booze and potato chips. It's tough to blame him though. Two hundred bucks doesn't go that far these days. I haven't seen him since, but I think about him a lot. I really regret how it happened, but what choice did I have?

Maybe Joey was right and I'm really just mean. Still, whenever I see a dog sniffing around in the bushes I run it off and I go and look and I hope it's not him.

Lost and Found Love

Lost Love:

I lost my love. I didn't even notice at first. I really liked Emily still and same thing with most of the people I'd loved.

Emily noticed, though. She said it dawned on her gradually, because I still kissed her and rubbed her arm and had sex with her and stuff, but it was clear something wasn't right.

Emily asked me straight up if I still loved her. I said of course I did, but it wasn't true and Emily didn't believe me.

It was the first time I knew I didn't love her and I was surprised. I felt around in all my pockets for it, but my love wasn't there.

I waited until Thursday night when Emily was out at the gym and I turned the place upside down looking for my love. I didn't find it, though.

A week later, Emily said she knew I was lying. She said if I really still loved her, I'd show her. She said she needed me to show her. I said that was ridiculous. I said love wasn't about garish, meaningless displays and Emily left me.

Emily didn't take a thing, except for her clothes and the stand mixer. I asked Emily not to go, and she said she didn't want to be with a guy who didn't love her. I told her she was making a big deal out of nothing, and Emily said she thought love was a pretty big deal.

I got on all right without Emily. I missed hanging out with her sometimes, but it wasn't like I loved her.

Found Love:

I found my love a year after Emily left, when the drain backed up and dumped sewage all over the bathroom floor. I called in a plumber and he said he'd never seen anything like it.

The plumber snaked the main drain and pulled up all this sludge and then there was a large sucking sound and fwoomp, my love spat up out of the drain and onto the floor, twisted and knotted and covered in shit. The plumber had no idea what it was. He said let him get rid of that for me, but I said no. I said I wanted to hang onto it as a memento. The plumber said he thought I was shit nuts, but if I wanted to keep it, that was up to me.

I washed my love in the bathtub and unknotted it and untwisted it and hung it on the shower-curtain rod to dry. In the morning, I picked up my love and I felt it all and I thought about Emily and there was an ache and a lump in my throat.

I called Emily right away. When she said hello, I launched into all this stuff about how I'd been careless to lose my love, but now I had it back I'd take care of it. I said I knew I couldn't make everything right, but I still loved her and I'd show her everyday if she wanted.

I talked so fast that the poor woman on the other end couldn't tell me that she wasn't Emily and she'd only had the phone number since May.

I sent Emily an email. I thought it was all too much for an email, so I just said that I really needed to speak with her.

LOST AND FOUND LOVE

Emily wrote me back that there wasn't really anything to talk about. She said she wasn't bitter so much as she'd moved on. She said she'd gone to Paris to study for a semester after we broke up, and she'd met somebody there and decided to stay.

I asked Emily if I could come and see her and she said she didn't think it was a good idea. I said I really did love her, and Emily said then it really wasn't a good idea.

I went to see Emily anyway. I sent her an email from an internet café in Paris and she asked if I was fucking nuts showing up like that. I begged her to let me see her, since I was there, and she said okay.

We met by the Eiffel Tower and these black guys kept trying to sell me two key chains for a Euro. I told Emily that it seemed clichéd to meet at a giant monument like the Eiffel Tower instead of in some café or restaurant and Emily said she liked it, because it made it easier for her to just walk away.

I said she couldn't walk away after I'd travelled thousands of kilometres to see her. Emily said of course she could, because she'd told me not to come.

I told Emily I loved her. I told her about how I'd lost my love. I said I didn't know how it had happened, but it had happened and it wouldn't happen again, and anyway, I loved her and I'd prove that I loved her everyday.

Emily said she hadn't been up the Eiffel Tower yet and she wanted to go, so we did. We went up to the second level and we walked towards the edge and she told me to jump. She said she was seeing somebody else and if I really loved her, I'd jump, because otherwise her life was too complicated.

I said okay, because I really loved Emily. I got out on the ledge and I jumped. I heard Emily scream and then I saw that she'd jumped too.

On the way down, I asked Emily what the hell she'd jumped for, and she said for love.

Childhood Memories

Sometimes my friends talk about their childhoods. It always starts with "when I was a kid," or "when we were kids." It never bothered me until my friend Donnie, who I've known since forever, said to me, "you never talk about your childhood." And even then it didn't bother me until I tried to think of an instance where I had and I couldn't.

I thought about when I was a kid. I tried to think of a story about something that happened, but I couldn't. I know I was a kid. I went to Severn Avenue Public School until the end of grade six and then I went to D Roy Kennedy. I can name most of my teachers – of course it helps that I had Mrs Rogers three years in a row – and a lot of my classmates. I just can't think of a single thing that happened.

Lately people have been coming up to me and telling me how they've always wanted to write a kids' book. Complete strangers mostly. I don't know why.

I've thought about this too, and I've realized that I can't even remember what it's like to be a kid. And I did some more thinking and I can't remember what it was like to be a teenager although I can tell you that Doug Anderson was student council president two years in a row. I can't remember my twenties either. I got married when I was twenty-nine and that's supposed to be memorable, but apparently not for me.

Even my thirties are fading and I'm only just forty. I got divorced when I was thirty-three and I only kind of remember that.

Maybe I just haven't done anything worth remembering. But lately I've been looking in people's eyes and I think maybe they can't remember either and they're just making it up. I wouldn't swear to it though.

Baseball

Sometimes when she's lying beside you in bed, or on your lap on the couch and you know she's asleep, you say "I love you," to her.

You say it to her face too. After awhile that's easy. "I love you," is just something you say to each other. It's when she's asleep that it's hard. Then you have to look at her and think about it and mean it.

When you say it and she's asleep, you feel good. All warm and fuzzy. You married her because you could say, "I love you," while she slept. Why she married you is a mystery, because she never falls asleep second or wakes up first.

One night you're on the couch watching the ball game and she's asleep with her head on your lap and the Yankees homer and you don't say, "I love you," you say, "Fuck. Why do they even bring him in to pitch? They could do better with the kid selling the crackerjacks." You're not sure they still make crackerjacks, but it's what you say.

She wakes up. She looks up at you and you smile and stroke her hair and say, "I love you."

"I love you," she says and falls back asleep. You look down at her and smile, but you don't say, "I love you." You'll never say it again while she sleeps.

You figure it's okay, because she's asleep so she doesn't know. It kind of is. You still hang out and you still fuck and you still say, "I love you," to each other. But sometimes when she's asleep you look at her and you want to cry because you can't say it. And sometimes when she's awake she gets a look in her eyes and you wonder if she really was asleep all those times, or if she wasn't and now she wonders why you never say, "I love you" anymore when you think she's asleep.

Winners

Jack Nelson was living in a room at the YMCA in downtown Toronto when he invented his game, and now he's rich as Croesus. That's because people keep playing the game even though they can't win. It's not that the game's rigged. It's not. It's just that it can't lose.

The beauty of the game is that it looks like it can lose. Jack Nelson advertised it as a game that couldn't lose and anywhere you can play it, it's called "The Game That Can't Lose." People take it as a challenge. They don't believe that the game can't lose. They believe that nobody's beaten the game so far, but they all think that they can be the first. That's why Jack Nelson's rich as Croesus.

Poker, blackjack, even slots have taken a back seat at casinos. They're not nearly the money winners they were before Jack Nelson invented his game. Jack Nelson licenses casinos to use his game, so he gets a share of every dollar they take in, and they take in a lot of dollars because casinos are paying out somewhere between a hundred thousand and a million to one and that draws players. It may as well be a billion to one though, because nobody's won it yet.

Jack Nelson says that wasn't his goal. He says his goal was actually the reverse. He says his goal was to show people the folly of gambling and the folly of letting other people control our lives. He says he thought his game would stop people from playing, because they'd see the pointlessness of it. He says he's a revolutionary and his goal was always to restore equality between the masses and the power structure. Now Jack Nelson's rich as Croesus, though and that's richer than Trump or Buffet or anyone else, but he hasn't done anything to help the masses.

IBM is working on a computer to beat the game. "We beat chess and we beat Jeopardy. We'll beat this too," an IBM spokesman said. People thought IBM would have it solved in a few weeks, but it's been a year and a half and they don't have it yet.

There was someone who said they'd solved it. A widowed pensioner in Drumheller Alberta. She called her son and told him that she'd solved it. "I just need a ride. We can start in Vancouver and go across the country and take down every casino in Canada," she said, but the son thought his mom had lost it and he hung up on her.

This woman put an ad on Craigslist looking for a driver. She offered the driver ten percent of her winnings.

I don't know whether or not she'd actually solved the game, because they found her dead at the side of the highway a half-hour outside of Edmonton.

Jack Nelson says he had nothing to do with it. "It was probably the driver, and the driver's probably already tried her tactic. The tactic won't have worked, because the game can't be beat. This is sick and wrong though. My point was to empower the proletariat. Remember, I was living at the YMCA in downtown Toronto when I invented this game. It saddens me," he said.

His autobiography is due out next April and he spends most of it talking about how he's trying to make the world a better place. He claims over and over that it was never about making money. It's going to be called: "Losing Everything: Why We Need to Empower the Masses". It sounds like a really shitty poli-sci book.

I know the title because I'm writing the book. Jack Nelson's paying the agency. The agency's paying me twelve bucks an hour and the book is going to be a best seller in less than a month even if the critics pan it.

Fortunately, I got paid a lot more for the old woman in Drumheller Alberta. I don't know if she really knew how to beat the game. When I asked her about it she said, "It's so simple when you think about it. I'm amazed that no one else has figured it out," but she wouldn't tell me how to do it. Even when I pulled out the gun she wouldn't tell me, so I calculated the odds that she'd actually solved the game and I took the sure money.

Geography Class

My geography teacher when I was in grade nine was Miss Wallach. Miss Wallach was maybe two years out of teachers' college. She was hot. I thought about her all the time.

Miss Wallach was even hotter than Lina, who I'd masturbated to since grade six when I didn't even know what I was doing. I set up a table in one of my work books and rated them in seven different categories. Miss Wallach beat Lina in every category. After that, I only thought about Miss Wallach when I masturbated.

I developed a scenario where I deliberately bombed a test, maybe I'd get one question right. That way Miss Wallach would ask to see me alone after class. When we were alone, I'd impress her with how much I actually knew. Miss Wallach would be mad, but not too mad.

"You shouldn't have done that, but I think I know why you did it. I hope it's worth it," she'd say and then she'd spank me.

The first few times, that's when I came. Later on, it evolved. She'd hike up her skirt and make me eat her pussy and then we'd fuck on one of the desks. It would become a regular thing.

Miss Wallach usually wore tight, thigh length skirts. I imagined she didn't wear panties in class and she'd flash me her snatch when no one else was watching.

It took me most of the year, but I finally worked up the nerve to bomb a test. Miss Wallach asked me to stay after class, but nothing else went like I'd imagined. She let me do a retest and I got seventy-four, which wasn't as high as I'd hoped.

Fifteen years later Miss Wallach was on TV being arrested. She'd been charged with twenty-two counts of sexual abuse and sexual interference involving minors.

My girlfriend Greta saw her on the six o'clock news. I'd moved into Greta's place about three months before that.

"Hey, did you see this?" Greta said.

I hadn't seen it, but it was the lead story on the local news for an entire week. They brought in psychologists and teachers and experts on child sexual abuse and victims of child sexual abuse. One of the victims was Corky. In fact Corky was the one who'd started the scandal by coming forward. A whole bunch more followed suit. They'd all been in grade nine when Miss Wallach had fucked them.

Corky'd been in my class. We'd been friends. He'd been a head shorter than me and he'd had a pot-belly and acne and he wasn't that smart. On TV the acne was gone, but he still had a pot-belly and he still wasn't that smart.

Corky's story sounded almost exactly like how I'd imagined being with Miss Wallach.

Miss Wallach pled guilty. She'd done it. That hurt. I watched Corky and a couple of experts talking about it and all I could think was what did Corky have that I didn't.

"Hey, didn't you go to her school?" Greta said.

"I was in her class. I was in Corky's class too."

"And she never did anything to you?"

"No."

"You're lucky. I hope they lock that manipulative bitch up for a long time," Greta said.

"Yeah."

In the morning I called in sick to work. By noon I had all of my stuff out of Greta's place.

The Compass

I lost my moral compass. It fell out of my pocket while I was running across the street against traffic. It got run over by an Audi.

The compass was a gift from my parents when I turned six. My parents were working class. Not broke, but they didn't have a lot of money. Still, they didn't skimp when they bought that gift. It survived being run over by an Audi. It wasn't a little coupe, either; it was the wagon.

The back tire of the car hit the compass full on, rolled over it and shot it straight into the air with the face staring at me. I've got twenty-ten vision. There wasn't a scratch on the thing.

I started to go back for the compass. It was a gift and I'd become attached to it. Dumb fucking luck. It dropped right through the sewer grate at the side of the road. It was just barely small enough to go through and only on its side. It was a one in a million shot, maybe one in a billion.

I wasn't happy about losing it. I'd had that compass for twenty-two years. It was an extension of me. Sometimes those are the breaks, though. I thought about replacing it, but I had no idea where to go to get a moral compass. I tried the internet, but even it didn't know. Them and Lowney's Peanut Butter Cups. You can find out about anything on the internet except moral compasses and Lowney's Peanut Butter Cups.

Not having a moral compass wasn't a big adjustment at first. My work, my friends and my family were all familiar territory and I could navigate them pretty well. It's amazing how predictable daily life is.

It was when my routines were broken that I had trouble. The first place I noticed a problem was dating. I felt awkward dealing with women because I couldn't figure out what was appropriate. I met a woman at a bar one night and I really wanted her. She was interested in me, but I got too aggressive and she slapped me in the face and stormed out. I still really wanted her, but I let her go. I'm not stupid.

I went home. The woman had slapped me really hard, and my cheek still stung. I put on some old clothes and I dug up a flashlight and some batteries and I went down to the spot where I'd lost my compass.

I pulled up the sewer grate. It must've weighed a hundred pounds, maybe a hundred and fifty. I left it lying at the side of the street and climbed down the ladder. I'd never tried dunking the compass, so I didn't know whether or not it would float. It felt like it was too heavy to float, but sometimes it's hard to tell these things.

I turned on the flashlight and hunted around the floor of the sewer. The weather had been dry and the water was only three or four inches deep.

I spent a while down there searching through the water and silt, probably a half hour and then I saw a second light shining from the hole.

"What the hell are you doing down there?" a voice said.

I looked up. It was a cop. I decided to lie. If I told him the truth, he'd haul me in. Then a psychologist would question me and they'd find out I had no moral compass of my own.

"I dropped my wedding ring down here. If I don't find it my wife'll kill me," I said.

"Yeah, I hear that. You're not allowed down there though, sir," he said, but he came down and helped me look for half an hour.

"It doesn't look like we're going to find it. Have you got insurance?" he said.

"Yeah."

"So it'll be okay. Your wife'll be pissed, but she'll get over it, and now you'll have a good story to tell."

"Yeah, I guess so. I'd better get home."

"Do you want me to fill out a report for you, for the insurance company?" the cop said.

"Nah, it's okay."

"Really, I don't mind."

I let him fill out the report, but I didn't submit a claim, because the insurance company knew I wasn't married. The event was instructive though. The cop had just believed what I'd said and he made a living dealing with criminals.

I practiced lying and manipulating people. As long as I was careful, it was a good way to get what I wanted.

I managed to get promoted twice by framing two different coworkers. I did it up right. It wasn't just my word against theirs. I carefully crafted and planted the evidence first. It pissed off those coworkers, but they got fired anyway for what I said they'd done. The second time it happened, the guy threatened to kill me in front of the entire office. I pursued it in court and he wound up with two years in prison.

I met Clara around the time my coworker went to jail. We fell in love and got married. It was easy, because I could do what worked without having to worry about what was right.

A year after we got married Clara got pregnant and we told friends and family. After we told my parents, my dad pulled me aside.

"You lost the compass we gave you, didn't you?" he said.

"The damn thing never pointed north anyway," I said.

"Listen to me son. You're defective. You can't tell right from wrong. It's not your fault. It's inherited. I'm the same way. It missed your sister, thank god. It's more common in boys, but there are women with the same defect."

"So are you saying my kid could be defective?"

"It doesn't matter. You can't raise a kid without a moral compass."

"I'm getting by okay. I'm doing better than I ever did when I had the stupid compass."

"Yeah, but you're a dick. Clara's noticed, you know. She's been talking to your sister. She's starting to figure out that something's wrong. Listen, you need to find yourself a new compass."

"Alright, let's say I do. Where do I get one?"

"Unfortunately the guy who made them died when you were eleven and he didn't leave a successor or a blueprint or anything. You'll have to steal one from somebody."

THE COMPASS

"How do I do that? What do I just mug people until I find one with a compass on them?"

"I have one. You'll have to kill me for it. I can't be like that, not in front of your mother or your sister and especially not in front of a grandchild."

"You're fucking nuts old man," I said.

Clara and I went home. I watched her. I looked for a sign that she knew. I thought that I could see it. She seemed uncomfortable. We went to bed and she seemed restless.

It must have been when I'd taken the money from that homeless guy. He'd dropped it all over the sidewalk. There'd been a couple of fives and some coins, enough for a good lunch. The money was clearly fair game, but I saw the look on Clara's face.

"Last week, with that homeless guy. I'm sorry Clara. I don't know what I was thinking. I just wasn't myself at that moment," I said.

"I know," she said.

I fell asleep, but I woke up at four and had to piss. Clara wasn't in bed. She wasn't home. I called my dad.

"She left me dad. Clara left me," I said.

"There's only one way you can fix it," he said.

I met my dad by the Ottawa River at four-thirty in the morning. We stripped off our clothes and he put the compass in his shoe. We swam out to where it was over our heads and I drowned my dad. He struggled. Even though he was over sixty and he was a head shorter than me, he was hard to hold down.

Eventually he stopped struggling and I swam back to shore. On the last leg, as I walked through the shallows to the beach, I stubbed my toe. I reached down and picked up my compass. After four years it had migrated to the shallows of Westboro beach.

It still worked. The face was fogged up, but I could tell the mechanism was still good. I held onto my compass and I realized what I'd done. I cried. I got dressed and I took my dad's compass out of his shoe and I raced home.

I took a shower and put on fresh clothes. I called Clara's parents and they said they had no idea where she was. I called my sister and she said that Clara had left the city.

"I need to track her down."

"I don't think that's a good idea," my sister said.

"I love her."

"She knows. I told her all about it."

"I've got something that she needs for the baby. It's really important."

"She's having an abortion this afternoon, after her plane lands. I'm sorry."

"What the fuck? She can't just kill our child without telling me. Where is she?"

"Sorry," my sister said and then she hung up on me.

I put down the phone and cried. I cried so hard that I threw up. I thought about my dad and I threw up again. What if my mom or my sister knew what I'd done and they turned me in? I saw my father's face lifeless and bobbing in the Ottawa River and I was sick a third time.

THE COMPASS

I thought about throwing away the compasses. Without them, the images wouldn't bother me, but I didn't think it was fair. At least to my father.

I took a hammer and a screwdriver and then a drill to my father's compass. It took me two weeks, but I managed to break the thing open. Now comes the task of figuring out how it works. If I can do that then I can make new ones. People talk all the time these days about the lack of moral compasses. There's a market out there for them, so I should be able to make good money and then my father's death won't have been for nothing.

The Tits of a High School Girl

Johnny Old called Elisa a slut. Or a tramp. Elisa. I wasn't there, but everybody said he said it. I mean, what could I do? I remember the day I walked into Mrs Mueller's class on the Tuesday after Labour Day and there she was. Her tits weren't as developed as Emily's. Emily had fantastic tits, like a high school girl. But Elisa had this curly red hair and these long legs and she even looked good with braces. So what could I do?

It didn't surprise me. Everybody knew Johnny Old was a dick. He was also the only kid in the class as big as me, the only kid in the class near as big as me. Johnny had blonde hair and a sneer and he was good at sports. We were too big for our age. I was awkward. Johnny Old wasn't.

I was scared shitless. I did okay in fights usually, because I was bigger than the guy I was fighting. Not this time. But he called Elisa a slut or a tramp, so what could I do? I walked up to him in the schoolyard after class was over for the day and I pushed him in the chest.

"What the fuck's your problem?" he said.

We both had people around. Johnny Old's were cooler. I punched him right in the face. I'd never been the tough kid, but then until that year I'd gone to a school where there were a lot of fights and Johnny Old would've been a pussy.

He put me in a headlock. I flailed uselessly. "Take it back," I said.

"What?" Johnny Old eased his grip a little and I managed to pull free. I punched him in the stomach.

"Take it back."

"What the fuck are you talking about?"

"You called Elisa a slut, or a tramp."

He caught me with a right across the side of my head. It hurt. I swung with my left. I was a lefty. I missed.

"I didn't mean it," he said. "I misspoke. I meant she's a whore."

I jumped at him. Johnny Old was a dick. Everybody knew he was a dick. I knocked him down and landed on top. It wasn't as well known that Johnny Old was a pussy. He kneed me in the balls once and I held firm. I put my forearm on his throat. He kneed me in the balls twice and threw me over.

"The whole class has felt her up, except you. Even the girls have felt her up," Johnny Old said.

I was on my back, but I hit him a good shot with my left and made his lip bleed. It pissed him off. He started swinging. I covered my head and did my best to fend him off. The entire grade six class was there and some of the grade sevens and eights too.

"Leave him alone," a girl's voice said. I looked through Johnny Old's flailing arms and the press of bodies and saw Elisa with her red hair and braces. Johnny Old didn't stop, but Nathan and Souleiman pulled him off.

We split up and went home. I guess I lost, but Johnny Old didn't make me bleed.

The next morning, in the middle of Souleiman's book report, Johnny Old and I got taken out of class and sent down to the vice principal's office. Mr Savage was the vice principal. He was tall and skinny. His right arm looked like a doll's. His hand always just rested in his pocket and his arm swayed uselessly back and forth when he moved. There was lots of speculation over whether or not it was his real arm, but we never found out for sure.

Mr Savage waved at two chairs with his left hand. Johnny Old and I sat. "I expect better of you two," Mr Savage said.

"He started it," Johnny Old said.

Mr Savage was a scary man to get called before. He didn't yell or scream, but he knew everything. He was like the CIA or something, and you always suspected a mole, but you never knew who it was.

"Why did he start it?" Mr Savage said.

"Because he ..." I said.

"I wasn't talking to you," Mr Savage said.

"I don't know why he started it," Johnny Old said.

"You have no idea at all? Who starts a fight for no reason at all?"

"I don't know. He does, I guess."

"You didn't call a young woman a slut and a whore?" Mr Savage said.

"No," Johnny Old said, but there was a long pause first and anybody could tell he was lying.

"And you," Mr Savage turned to me. "What's it got to do with you?"

"Well, it's not right to say stuff like that. Elisa's not a slut." My face got red when I said her name.

"You're right. He shouldn't be saying things like that. Do you think that warranted fighting him?"

"Yes. I don't know."

"You don't know if violence is appropriate?"

"No."

"No you don't know?"

"No, it's not."

"You will both report here for recesses and lunch today and tomorrow," Mr Savage said.

The next week, I saw Johnny Old and Elisa together around the back of the school. He wasn't feeling her up or anything, they were just talking. The week after that, Elisa got her braces off. I don't know, but somehow she looked less attractive without them. Her red hair didn't bounce the same way and her long legs were kind of skinny and her tits weren't as developed as Emily's. Emily had fantastic tits, like a high school girl.

Real

I realized a couple of years ago that my life was a movie. I wasn't sure when it started filming. The movie might have covered my entire life and I was just slow catching on, but it might only have been about my adult years. I figured either way it would take a lot of editing, because who wants to spend their entire lives in a movie theatre. Even a couple of years would feel long. Especially because it's not an action movie. It's one of those slow moving independent films.

I had no idea who'd written the script, but I figured they couldn't be really A-list. Sometimes the dialogue was stilted, and there were virtually no special effects. Nothing's blown up around me. Even the drama is low key.

My cousin's in the movie. He's the minor character that's everyone's favourite. He pops up regularly and always in the same spot. You know he's symbolic of something, but you're not sure of what.

I figured my wife was probably pretty popular too. I really like her, but she's in it a lot.

My cousin's ten years younger than me. His dad's ten years younger than my dad too, so we didn't see a lot of each other growing up.

As kids, I guess we came close to breaking even. When I was eleven, he threw up on me, and when I was fifteen, I knocked out two of his teeth while we were playing soccer at our grandparents' cottage, but he was going to lose those teeth anyway.

The reason he's in the movie is he works at the bar at the top of my street. I don't go into the bar much, but I walk by it all the time. Most of the time he's leaning against the wall with a coffee in one hand and a cigarette in the other.

He's been working there for two years. For two years I've walked by and stopped to talk to him. We talk about life and family and shit.

About a year ago, I became suspicious that my cousin was involved in the production. I wondered if he was the writer/director. Lots of writers and directors cast themselves in bit parts, so it kind of made sense.

But that's not it at all. It turns out that Louis is the star and I'm the bit character and my wife's just in the credits as "cousin's wife."

When I think about it, it fits. Louis works in a bar. It's a good location for a movie about life. Louis is blonder too, and he's still finding himself, and all the stars smoke anyway, especially when they're doing independent films.

I'm happy for Louis, but it kind of sucks for me. It means that most of my life is just background for my character so that my scenes with Louis are more convincing. It's not essential to the plot, which means it'll be among the first things eliminated if the movie runs into money troubles.

Hopefully I at least come off well. I don't think I've done too badly. As long as they cut those scenes from childhood.

It Couldn't Have Happened to a Nicer Guy

Xiu Li is my ex-girlfriend. It used to be Susie growing up. The Wall Street Journal recently called her the most important business figure under forty in the entire world and I'm nobody, so people don't really believe me when I tell them she's my ex-girlfriend. Even still, she has aides call me and tell me to stop mentioning it. But it's true and we were in love. When she was Susie. Before her and Todd.

We grew up with Todd in Richmond just outside Vancouver. He lived around the corner from me and down the street from Xiu Li. Xiu Li's relationship with Todd is kept kind of quiet now too, but I remember it because she dumped me for him.

Todd got rich by inheriting his great uncle's company. The great uncle didn't like his own kids, but he wanted to keep the company in the family, so he passed everything on to Todd who he'd met like twice. We were twenty-seven then.

Todd ended up being a good choice. He doubled the company's holdings in two years. The Economist profiled him as an up and comer. There was a line in the article where some executive who'd been with the company for thirty-eight years said, "All the success Todd's enjoyed, it couldn't have happened to a nicer guy."

Xiu-Li and I were living in Toronto at the time. She was working as a reporter for the Toronto Star. She read the article and showed it to me.

"Huh. I always thought Todd was a prick," I said and Xiu-Li shrugged.

Xiu-li did shitty local stories and a weekly style column for the Toronto Star. She took the article in the Economist to her editors and told them that she'd grown up with Todd. They put her on a plane to Seattle to go and interview him. She was supposed to be gone for four nights.

On the fourth night, she called me.

"I think I'm going to stay out here," she said.

"But what about your job?"

"I'll find something new out here. My editors said they'll put in a good word for me. I kind of miss the coast."

"What about me? I can't just up and leave. I've got a job too, and we don't have a lot of money Susie."

"I'm staying with Todd," she said. She hung up on me and that was the end of four years. I called her up and tried to talk her into coming back, but she wouldn't come to the phone.

Eleven months after Xiu Li left me, Todd died in a boating accident. Todd had changed his will so that Xiu Li got everything. She took the business and merged it with a huge Chinese firm. She stayed on as CEO and had a controlling interest. Now The Wall Street Journal says she's the world's most important business person under forty, maybe of any age.

I ran into her a couple of years ago in a Starbucks in Vancouver. It was right around the time of the merger. She smiled at me.

"You were right. Todd was always a prick. Even in kindergarten. That's the point. You remember the snake that he put down Alison Miller's pants and the time he made Tommy Rosen lick dirt off his shoe? I never would have figured it out if it wasn't for you," she said.

Now she has aides call me and tell me not to talk about her and me, and sometimes I feel like I'm being followed.

All the articles I read about her say that none of this could have happened to a nicer person, and that makes me sad, because she used to be nice.

The Big Picture

There's this painting at the Met called The Big Picture. It's huge. It takes up the entire long wall in the hall that it's in. It's not a mural, though. It's a canvas, and it's in a cheap, plastic, black frame. The frame looks like something you'd get at Ikea only bigger. When the Met unveiled The Big Picture, the critics all called it revolutionary.

The Big Picture isn't just a painting. It shifts forms as you look at it, like those computer generated pictures from the nineties, only you don't have to unfocus your eyes.

Supposedly everyone who looks at The Big Picture sees something different, or maybe they just focus on a different spot in the painting. When people look at it, they see themselves, but usually just in a corner and often it takes a while for them to spot themselves. You'd think something like that would make people feel insignificant, but it doesn't.

The people who see the painting say it's transformative. They report being happier and more hopeful than before they saw it. The effect is so strong that employers all over the world have organized and paid for their workers to go to New York and see it.

Nobody knows who created the painting. It was donated to the Met anonymously. That really pissed Edgar off. Edgar hated The Big Picture and he hated the fucker who'd created it even though he'd never seen it.

Nina, who'd been Edgar's best friend since university, had seen The Big Picture nineteen times because her girlfriend lived in New York. Nina thought it was the greatest work of art ever created.

"You can't hate it. You've never even seen it," she said. She said it all the time. Other people Edgar knew said it too. Some of them were even artists. People Edgar figured should understand.

He got so sick of hearing it that he finally went to see The Big Picture. He crashed at Nina's girlfriend's for three days. Each day he went to the Met and stood in the hall and stared at The Big Picture. It was brilliant. Edgar couldn't get a handle on why, but after he saw it, he felt better.

Time went by, though and the feeling faded. He was still stuck painting houses and trying to sculpt in his spare time. When he'd seen The Big Picture it had all made sense. The things he did served a purpose. He was part of something bigger and he was working towards an end. After, he wasn't at the end. He was still doing the things to get him there.

Edgar got on a bus and went back to New York for a fix. He figured another look would make him feel better again, but it didn't. He stared at the painting and he stared at the people around him staring at the painting and he didn't feel better. He stayed in the hall until the Met closed and two three hundred pound security guards came and threw him out.

When Edgar got home he got up in the morning and went and painted houses. When he came home and he wasn't too tired he sculpted and he hated his life.

THE BIG PICTURE

A week after Edgar got back from New York the second time, he started work on a new sculpture. It took him six years to finish the sculpture, because he had to figure out the right combination of materials and the right shape.

Nina moved to New York to be with her girlfriend and to be close to The Big Picture. She tried to go see the painting every day.

One day when she went to see The Big Picture, there was a tiny sculpture on the floor in front of it in the left hand corner. The sculpture was called The Small Mind. Nina had a hard time getting a handle on the sculpture, but it made her angry. It reminded her of how her life was, how she was working so hard and all her money was going to rent and her museum membership and how she hardly had sex and how she went to see the same stupid painting every day to try and find meaning in her otherwise empty life.

Edgar made a mint off the sculpture. The Met wouldn't say how much they paid for it, but it was a lot and Edgar made sure his name was on a plaque at the base of the sculpture.

The critics love The Small Mind even more than they love The Big Picture and the people keep going to the Met and standing in that room. When you walk in all you see is The Big Picture. You don't even notice the little sculpture in the corner, but gradually it draws you in.

People go to see The Small Mind and they leave pissed off as hell, but they talk about it, and they keep going back to see it. The government is worried. They've tried to have The Small Mind removed. So have certain religious groups. A French woman who claims she created The Big Picture says that one or the other of them has to go, but they're both still there.

Both houses of Congress have passed a bill ordering the removal of The Small Mind and the president's signed it into law, but there was a massive protest and they had to back down. Nina was at the protest. She's at the Met every day. If she can, she goes twice a day.

All You Need Is Love

People have been saying for centuries that all you need is love, but Lisa was the first to prove it. Some people thought she was kind of an uppity bitch for not needing anything else, but it didn't bother her and most people loved her.

Lisa wasn't crazy. She wasn't in your face about how she only needed love. If you invited her to a dinner party she'd show up in something appropriate and she'd eat and stuff. She just didn't need to.

Lisa was my older brother Ron's girlfriend. Ron really loved Lisa. Lisa loved Ron too, but it always felt like he loved her more. I kind of think he did. I loved Lisa more than I loved Ron and he was my brother. The thing with Lisa was that she loved everyone and most people loved her back. It was like she'd worked out a love equation and love wasn't an effort anymore.

We used to hang out a lot, the three of us. When Ron met Lisa we were both living with our parents. Ron was thirty and I was twenty-five. When I met Lisa I couldn't figure out why a woman like that would date a thirty year old who lived with his parents.

Ron couldn't either. He figured it was only a matter of time, so he got his shit together. Three weeks after he and Lisa met, he had his own apartment and a job that paid him seventy grand a year.

I'd go over to Ron's place and the three of us would play video games or watch movies. On the weekends we'd go out drinking together and Lisa would try to fix me up with women. Sometimes it bugged Ron how much time I spent with them, but Lisa liked having me around and neither of us could say no to her.

Ron and Lisa were together for four and a half years. Lisa was pretty normal in public, but in private she was kind of weird. She never got hot or cold. She'd go outside in the middle of winter and roll in the snow completely naked. Ron swore that she once went a month without eating or drinking anything and she gained a pound.

What did the two of them in was that Lisa liked sex. "It's a physical expression of love," she said. Lisa didn't need sex. She gave it up for four months once at my request, except to have sex with Ron.

Ron had no idea about Lisa. Lisa didn't need sleep. That's how she did it. Sometimes she'd go to bed with Ron and fall asleep, because she didn't need to be awake either. Usually, though, she'd get up when Ron was asleep. Some nights she'd sit with me on the couch and we'd play video games and talk. Some nights she'd go out and meet somebody and fuck them. She loved everyone she fucked and everyone she fucked loved her back.

Lisa was careful about it, because she knew Ron would be jealous. She only fucked people she was sure she'd never see again. She stayed off Facebook and Twitter and Flickr.

I wanted to fuck Lisa. I asked her once when I was drunk.

"I don't know that that's a good idea," she said. "All you need is love, but Ron hasn't accepted that yet. You haven't either. If I slept with you it could ruin both of you."

"He'll never know," I said.

"Of course he will. You'll feel guilty and you'll get drunk again and you'll blurt it out," she said.

We got ruined anyway. Ron worse than me. Ron decided to put some pictures of Lisa on his Facebook profile, and this guy he went to Connaught Public School with when he was six sent Ron a message saying he'd fucked his girlfriend. The guy told him that he loved Lisa and that Lisa had said she loved him.

Ron didn't really believe it, but he asked Lisa about it anyway. Lisa lied, but more people popped up on Facebook telling Ron they'd fucked his girlfriend.

Ron asked me if it was true. I lied, but I didn't lie well enough.

"All she needs is love my ass. That fucking little tramp. I'll kill her," Ron said.

"You can't. She loves you Ron. It's just that she loves other people too and they love her back."

"Yeah? Do you love her?"

"Yes."

"You fucker," Ron said.

We fought and Ron kicked the shit out of me, even though I was a head taller and in better shape. After, he took off. I figured he was going for Lisa, so I got up and went after him.

I caught up to Ron at his and Lisa's place. Ron had a knife in his hand and Lisa was lying on the floor bleeding like crazy.

"Jesus Ron!" I ran at my brother and he took off again. This time I let him go. I sat down on the floor beside Lisa and grabbed at her stomach where the blood was coming out.

"Damn it. Damn it. You can't die Lisa. I love you Lisa. You can't die. I'll kill that fucker. I'll find him and I'll kill him," I said.

"Don't. I'll be okay. I don't need blood. All I need is love. I have love. Even Ron still loves me," Lisa said.

She sat up. She took off her top. She grabbed a towel from the linen closet and she tied it around her stomach. Then she sat down on the couch and we played video games until the cops showed up. A neighbour had heard shouting and called 911. They broke down the door and they found Lisa's blood all over the floor. The towel she was wearing was covered in blood too.

They called an ambulance and then they went after Ron. Ron got as far as the US border. Lisa's blood was all over his clothes and the knife was on the passenger seat. They told Ron to get out of the car and he ran the gate. When they pulled him out of the car on the south side of the border, he had twenty-eight bullets in him.

That night was the last time I saw Lisa. She sent me a letter once to tell me she was okay and to say she still loved me and Ron. I still love her too, but it's different. I used to admire Lisa. I used to want to be like her, but not now. It's not natural to live like that.

BMX

"I'll make you a deal," my dad said. "If you can ride your sister's bike to the end of the street and back, I'll get you a BMX."

My bike was little and the front wheel was smaller than the back one and it still had the training wheels on it. My sister was three years older than me, so her bike wasn't like that. Her bike was too big for me. I couldn't even reach the pedals sitting down, but I rode it.

It took me two weeks of practicing. I had to stand up in front of the seat and the handlebars were far away and I was all stretched out. The bike wobbled back and forth the whole way.

After I did it, I told my dad. "I didn't see it," he said.

"Mom did. So did Carrie," I said.

"Well I didn't see it," he said, so I did it again while he watched.

"So can I get a BMX now?"

"We'll see."

Eight days later my dad was in a car accident on his way home from work. I still didn't have my BMX. My dad wound up in the hospital. The doctors said he was brain dead, but he kept breathing. I figured he kept breathing because of the BMX. You can't die without fulfilling a promise to your six year old.

My dad stayed unconscious throughout my entire childhood. They kept him on an IV and waited for him to stop breathing, but he didn't. After awhile they wanted permission to take out his IV. I think my mom would have let them, but she made the mistake of asking me and Carrie and my dad stayed on his IV.

In university I did biology and then I went to med school, because I wanted to find a way to bring my father back. When I was forty I managed to get his brain working and he regained consciousness. Everyone expected him to have severe brain damage, but he didn't.

He opened his eyes and said, "Who are you?"

"I'm your son."

"Aren't you six?"

"I was. You were in your thirties. A lot's happened since then. They wanted to pull your IVs and just let you die, but Carrie and I wouldn't let them."

I figured my dad would be grateful, but he wasn't. He started to babble about the afterlife.

"You weren't dead dad," I said.

"I know. Do you think I don't know? They reminded me everyday for what seemed like forever."

"You were out just under thirty-four years," I said.

"No wonder it felt like forever. You know they make you get a temporary pass and no matter how long you're there, you've got to renew it every week and nobody wants anything to do with you, because they know you're not dead. They can tell because you change over time and because you've got this stupid pass that you've got to show everywhere. Let me tell you, the afterlife's no hell, but at least when you're dead it's yours."

BMX

"Fascinating. You must not have been completely brain dead after all."

"It said brain dead on my temporary passes."

"Anyway dad, that's just where you were. When you go back, which won't be for awhile, you'll be in a better place. It's all because you never got me the BMX bike you promised me."

"What?"

"The BMX. You made me a deal. You said if I could ride Carrie's bike to the end of the street and back you'd get me a BMX."

"You wouldn't let them pull the plug because of a BMX?" my dad said.

"You were never plugged. You always breathed on your own. It was just IV hook ups."

"You're forty for Christ's sake. Can't you buy yourself a BMX bike?"

"That's not the point."

My dad lasted a year to the day. They tried to get him out of bed and rebuild his muscles, but he had no interest in it. He had no interest in my bike either.

The day he died I went out and bought a BMX. I've tried to ride it, but it's too small, so now it sits in the garage behind the snow tires.

Photographic Evidence

When I was twenty-six I went to Europe. France and Germany for three weeks. It was the first time I'd ever been out of Canada and the northern US. I spent most of my time in Paris and Berlin, but I saw some countryside too. I even went to Monaco and lost two hundred and fifty Euros playing blackjack. I didn't bring a camera.

When I came back people asked to see photos.

"I didn't bring a camera," I said.

"What the hell? How can you tell people you went somewhere and not bring back even one picture?" my friend Chris said.

A couple of years later I went to Italy for two weeks. My parents got me a digital camera as a Christmas present before I left.

"This time there are no excuses," my mom said.

I took the camera and I took the little stuffed Winnie the Pooh that my girlfriend had got me. I took pictures of Winnie the Pooh on monuments and stuff. I got him in the Coliseum and on a gondola in Venice, like people do with those travelling gnomes. I had no eye for photography, but at least Winnie the Pooh was photogenic. He wasn't one of those Disney Poohs with the red t-shirt. He was a Gund Pooh and he was furry instead of smooth.

I got back from vacation and I downloaded all the photos to my hard drive and showed them to my girlfriend. Nobody questioned whether or not they were real. My girlfriend even complained that I'd taken all these pictures of Winnie the Pooh and if I'd taken her then the photos would be of her instead, but I was afraid that people thought they were fake.

I became paranoid about it. I was only in one or two photos and I could have faked those. I could have faked my receipts and museum passes too. When I showed the photos to a new person, I watched their eyes to see if they were buying it.

I made sure not to touch up any of the photos, even the ones with red eye. But that's just how I would do my photos if I was going to fake them. I'd make some of them underexposed and some of them overexposed and even throw in a thumb somewhere.

My girlfriend broke up with me and I went to South America. I took an entire month. I did a backpacking tour through the Andes. I brought my camera, but I didn't use it much. I talked to everyone on the tour, though and I made sure I wound up in their photographs so they could be witnesses. I gave my email to a couple of people and asked them to send me photos. One girl actually did, but it didn't ease my paranoia.

I felt like I was just some guy popping up, like Where's Waldo. I figured memories weren't that reliable. It'd be easy to convince everybody I'd spoken to that it hadn't been me. I was just some guy from somewhere.

I started to doubt myself. Maybe I'd never left home. When I was a kid my mom told me I had an active imagination. My dad said overactive. What if I'd made the whole thing up? There's so much information now and you can do virtual tours and stuff without ever going anywhere. There was nothing I'd seen or learned I couldn't have gotten off of Wikipedia. Maybe I was insane.

I figured I needed to prove that I'd been places. I packed up Winnie the Pooh and went to Japan. I spent ten days and saw a Buddhist monastery and some cherry blossoms and then I jumped from the forty-fifth floor of a hotel in Tokyo. On the way down I started to think. What does a body prove?

Like In Roshomon

When I was seven my older sister's best friend was Tammy. Tammy's parents were divorced. She lived with her mom and her mom worked, so she came to our house after school.

One day Tammy took me and my friend Bobby into my sister's room. She made us strip naked and then she played with our cocks. She also kissed me on the lips, but she didn't kiss Bobby. My sister was there, but she just watched and didn't do anything.

After, Bobby went home and told his mom. We all got in trouble and Tammy stopped coming over to our house after school. My sister and I weren't allowed to talk about it.

Bobby's parents moved to another neighbourhood with a different school and they sent Bobby to see a psychiatrist. Bobby moving didn't bother me too much. Kevin and Shun and Chris were all better friends than Bobby.

After, I mostly didn't think about it. Not until I was thirty. When I was thirty, I ran into Tammy in a bar in Montreal. We talked. She was drunk and I got drunk and we went back to her place at three in the morning.

Tammy was thirty-four and she didn't take care of herself. She had huge bags under her eyes and she wore too much makeup and she had a bit of a gut, but she was still half-sexy. We sat on the couch and talked about when we were kids and she said she still thought about it a lot. She said she'd written up a script and she brought home younger guys and made them play me and if she could find a second one, she made the second one play Bobby.

It sounded sick, but it turned me on. We replayed the scene from her script and then we fucked and it was amazing. The only thing was that her script went exactly the way I remembered it. Even the dialogue was the same. Word for word when I thought about it.

I kept seeing Tammy even though I was in Ottawa. I'd go down once or twice a week. Pretty much every Friday. We'd re-enact our childhood and then we'd fuck. Sometimes we'd go out to a club first and we'd try to find people to play the part of Bobby or my sister. None of it bothered me, except that the script was word for word how I remembered it happening.

I mentioned it to Tammy one night. "We're kindred spirits Lou, that's all," she said.

I called up Bobby and told him. I still kept in touch with Bobby. We went for coffee every couple of months.

"You're what? Jesus man. That's sick, you know that, right? You've gotta get out of there. Stop seeing her," he said.

"You're missing the point Bobby. We remember what happened exactly the same. I mean the script. It's identical to what I remember. What do you remember?"

"I remember that it was unhealthy. My mom sent me to a psychiatrist after."

"Yeah, but your mom was always overprotective. You must have talked about the whole thing with the psychiatrist, though."

"That was twenty years ago."

"Twenty-two. But you must have talked about it."

"Sure, but I'm not talking about it with you."

I figured that was the end of it, but Bobby sent me an email two days later. In the email, he said the psychiatrist had made him write out what he remembered. He still had a copy of the journal he'd written it in for some reason. He scanned in the pages for me. It was faded and messy and there were a lot of spelling errors, but it was the same as Tammy's version. It wasn't just the dialogue that was the same. Even the stage directions and the descriptions of the room were the same.

I asked Tammy if she ever saw Bobby.

"No. I doubt I'd even know him if I fell over him now. I remember him being a fat, ugly, little shit of a kid. Why?" she said.

"You haven't seen him at all since that day?"

"Not that I know of. Why?" I told her about Bobby's journal. She shrugged. "So?"

"It doesn't bother you?" I said.

"Why should it?"

I kept seeing Tammy, but it started to feel weird. I asked my sister to meet me for coffee. We didn't talk much normally, but she agreed to meet me. I asked her what she remembered about the incident and she said not much. I showed her Bobby's journal and she said, "so?"

"Does it jibe with your memory?" I said.

"I guess so. It sounds about right."

"About right?"

"It's like I remember it, all right?"

"Exactly like you remember it?"

"It was more than twenty years ago."

"Yeah, but you remember it, right? And you remember it just like that, right?"

"Fuck off Lou."

In Roshomon everybody remembers what happened differently. That's how it's supposed to be. We were all stuck with exactly the same memory. It had to be some kind of conspiracy or brainwashing or something. Maybe something really terrible had happened and the adults didn't want us to know so they just programmed us. My mind ran through all kinds of shit.

I thought about it awhile and then one night I got Bobby and my sister to come with me to Montreal. Bobby knew why, but I lied to my sister. We went to Tammy's place and we all got drunk and went into the bedroom. We played out the scene without a script and everybody got their parts right.

After, Tammy and I fucked right in front of Bobby and my sister. Bobby sat there staring with his dick in his hands. He was so drunk he couldn't get it hard, and after he was sick. When Tammy came, my sister walked out and that's when it occurred to me: I'd remembered Bobby being circumcised.

IQ

When I was nine I took an IQ test. I scored okay.

"That's a good score, but remember, IQ tests aren't reliable indicators of intelligence," my mom and dad said.

That's not what they said when Cheryl was nine and took an IQ test. What they said when Cheryl was nine and took an IQ test was, "We always knew you were bright." Then we all went out to dinner and Cheryl got to pick where. Cheryl wanted to go to Red Lobster, so that's where we went even though I hate seafood.

I asked Miss Bellamy about it. Miss Bellamy was my teacher and she was Cheryl's teacher when Cheryl was nine.

"You got a good score," she said. "Don't try to compete with Cheryl. IQ's not that important. You know what's interesting? They say the oldest child gains ten IQ points just for being the oldest, and if something happens to the oldest, the next child gets those ten IQ points.

"But IQ's not important. The middle child is the conciliator. You're very good with the other children Patrick. You have a knack for getting along with people and that's very valuable."

I thought about what Miss Bellamy said and it seemed like a gyp to me. If IQ wasn't important then why did they send Cheryl to a special school for smart kids? And her IQ was more than ten points higher than mine. She didn't need those ten points. I needed those ten points. Without them, who knew what would happen to me. If Cheryl was any kind of a sister she'd give them to me, or at least split them between me and Joey.

I devised a plan to get rid of Cheryl. I wasn't as smart as her, but I took my time planning it out and setting it up and she wouldn't know it was coming.

The plan wasn't that complicated. There were woods across the street from our house and we used to play in them. There was a small ravine with a creek that ran through the woods. The creek bed was rock and the water was shallow and you could crack your head open if you fell hard enough. There were stories about a boy ten years ago who fell in and hit his head and died.

I worked after school for a week to make sure that this one spot beside the creek would give way if you stepped there. The slope was rocky there and all the rocks would go tumbling too. I also hid a big rock nearby just in case I had to go down and finish the job.

When it was all set up, I got Cheryl to stand right next to the spot. All I had to do was give her a little push and she'd go down. That's when it occurred to me that once Cheryl was gone maybe Joey would get the same idea. I'd have to find a way to take care of Joey too. And then my parents could always have more kids. I could spend the rest of my life drowning little brothers and sisters in the bathtub.

Who needed that? I pulled Cheryl away from the spot.

"Careful, those rocks look loose," I said.

Let Cheryl have to watch her back. I may not be smart like her, but that's okay. I'm the middle child. The middle child's easy. The pressure's off. All you have to do is smile and act friendly. I can do that.

Ordinary

There was nothing special about Tom. I knew Tom from the time we were three and he was ordinary. Mediocre down the line.

In grade four when we did IQ tests, he scored exactly a hundred, even though he was the middle class white kid they wrote the test for. He wasn't any hell at sports either.

And yet Tom was the most successful of any of us from the neighbourhood, man or woman.

It wasn't because of his magnetism, or ability with a crowd. His speech in grade ten about Pierre Trudeau's return to politics put half the class to sleep. It wasn't work ethic. Tom could be a lazy fucker.

Most of us who really knew Tom chalked it up to luck. Like the year we won the league hockey championships. Tom was on the third line. He only had two shifts in the whole third period of the championship game, but he scored the winner when Bobby McGuire drilled a slap shot from the point that hit Tom's stick while Tom was on his ass in front of the net.

Luck seemed to be the story of his life. Not a lot of people know it, but the only reason Tom got into McGill was that eighteen students declined acceptance to protest the firing of a popular professor. Luckily, Tom was eighteenth on the waiting list for his program. Tom muddled through four years with a dead-on C average and then went to work for Saint Lawrence Shipping.

Things went Tom's way again at Saint Lawrence Shipping. A month after he started there, the company's owner had a heart attack at a morning meeting of the executives. Apparently the owner had been a real shit and all the executives were real shits too. Nobody called the ambulance until lunch.

When the workers found out about the owner, they staged a coup. It was like when the imperial guard pulled Claudius from behind the curtain after Caligula was assassinated. The story goes that they found Tom in the break room sipping a coke and they sent him in to fire the entire executive.

It just kept going from there. Most people know Tom's story, more or less. He wound up controlling more than half of Canada's shipping industry with major shares of the US and European markets as well.

Maybe if Tom had been impossibly good looking or if he'd had a really intense stare or something, but most people described him as plain. He was six feet tall, which is above average, but nobody much seems to have noticed. When they measured him for his coffin his wife's response was, "really? I never thought he was that tall."

Nobody could ever find anything else to explain Tom's success, so they settled on luck. Even Tom claimed it was luck. In interviews he always talked about how he'd been lucky. He never said fortunate. It was luck that made Tom great.

Somehow that never felt quite right to me. Even as a kid it didn't feel right.

ORDINARY

When Tom died last week, it confirmed my suspicions. People say his luck ran out. That's how the media has framed it. "Lucky guy's luck runs out," as one particularly bad headline put it. Even Tom's official biographer has said that Tom's luck just ran out.

It can't be though, because Tom wasn't just deserted by luck. Tom died the unluckiest death I've ever heard of. His private jet got grounded due to a mechanical problem and he had to fly commercial. The guy in the seat next to him got drunk because he'd just split up with his wife. He passed out with a cocktail sword in his left hand.

The guy leaned over in his sleep and his head hit Tom's shoulder. He woke up disoriented and reached out with his left hand to where Tom was. He hit Tom in the face, accidentally stuffing the cocktail sword down Tom's esophagus. The esophagus and the trachea ruptured and the sword was stuck fast while Tom choked to death.

Tom would've been forty-six next month. That's pretty young nowadays. I don't know exactly what it was that made Tom so successful, but it wasn't luck. If you're lucky, you don't die like that.

Maybe it was destiny, or maybe Tom understood something that nobody else got. It's too bad it wasn't luck, because if he'd just been lucky that would have meant there was hope for everybody who was ordinary.

The Moment

I captured a moment one night in a bar. I'd never tried to capture a moment before. My memory's pretty good. Maybe that's why I never tried to capture a moment until that night in the bar, but that night I met a woman. She said her name was Molly. Molly was short. She had big eyes and long hair and thick, athletic legs and a round ass.

Molly and I shared a moment. It was in a bar and everyone knows those moments don't last, but I wanted it to.

I was twenty-six and so was Molly. I told Molly I needed to capture the moment and she said it could be done if I was serious.

"You have to be careful with moments, though. They don't take well to captivity. They're like chameleons. They change on you and you think they're not how they actually are."

Molly told me she knew. She said she worked for a department that was trying to represent the world the way it really was. She said they captured moments, actual moments, and stored them. She said moments were slippery. She said they all tried to escape. She said some of them, when they can't escape, get so twisted around that you can't use them and then you have to put them down.

I said I wanted the moment and I'd take the chance. Molly told me how to do it, but she said she wouldn't help. "Why not?"

"I don't want this moment to turn on me," she said.

I waited until the end of the night, like Molly said. I danced with her for a while, but I couldn't concentrate in her presence. Molly was intoxicating. I left her and went to the bar and ordered a coffee.

Molly said that you could see a moment if you knew what you were looking for, and you could. I picked up our moment pretty quickly. It floated around the room and danced with the men and women. It swirled through legs and over asses and it lingered in people's crotches.

Molly said that moments usually go out the back door. "A moment like that'll stick around until everybody's gone. Even the servers. Then it'll slip out the back."

She was right. I stayed at the bar watching the moment until they kicked me out. Then I went around back. One of the waiters saw me when he was taking out the trash. He threatened to call the cops if I didn't leave, so I walked out to the main street and counted to twenty before going back for the moment.

The moment came out around quarter to five. It was with a bunch of other moments that had been had by other people, but I recognized it right away. I jumped out from behind the dumpster and wrestled the moment to the ground and popped a plastic garbage bag over it. The other moments scattered and I took my moment home. It struggled the whole way, but it couldn't get out of the bag.

I didn't have anywhere else to put the moment, so I put it in the terrarium with the gecko.

I treated the moment pretty well at first. I let it out in my bedroom for an hour or so every day after work.

THE MOMENT

The moment was friendly. It wasn't at all like Molly described. It was playful. It showed me the way Molly moved. It showed me the sparkle in her eyes when she looked at me and the slight upturn in her nose and her crooked smile. It even got rid of the pimple on my chin.

After a couple of weeks, things with the moment started to change, though. The moment dwelled on stuff. On further reflection, it said. It pointed out how Molly hadn't given me her number to get in touch with her. It showed me how she'd told me how to capture the moment, but even though she was the expert, she hadn't helped.

The moment showed me the look that Molly gave to the bartender and how the bartender was better looking than I was. The pimple on my chin came back and it had a big whitehead. Then the moment showed me how Molly's mouth was crooked even when she didn't smile and it showed me how her left eyelid drooped and it showed me how she had a hot ass and strong thighs, but she also had a bit of a belly.

Six months after I captured the moment it came out and told me that Molly wasn't interested in me. It said six months was way too long if she was really interested. It said had I ever heard of an organisation capturing moments? I said no and it said of course not, there was no such organisation. It said Molly had made a lucky guess on how to capture it, and even if she had known what she was doing, she was clearly trying to get rid of me by distracting me with the moment.

I got pissed off and I shoved the moment into a Tupperware and sealed the lid. The moment begged me not to. It offered to help me find Molly if I'd just let it go, but I didn't. I shoved the Tupperware into a box and shoved the box into the back of my closet.

I didn't touch the moment for ten years. When I moved in with Alice, I threw the box in the back of the truck and when I unloaded it, I put it in the basement next to the furnace.

Things were good between me and Alice then, but they didn't stay that way. One night we had a huge fight. I said she was spending too much time with this guy Brent from work and she said, "You turn and stare at the ass of every girl you walk by." I called her a bitch and she called me a dick and then she went out.

Things might have been okay between us still, but after Alice left, I went to the basement and pulled out the moment. The moment let out a huge gasp when I opened the Tupperware and then it came out and I relived it. The moment wasn't bitter. It was actually really nice to me. It told me it believed that there was somebody for everybody and that you could see just by watching us that Molly and I were meant to be together.

After that, I took the moment out anytime I was alone. The moment made me happy. Things even got better between me and Alice for a bit. Then one morning when I wasn't paying attention, the moment got into the ducts. It slipped out through the cold air return in the bedroom and I never saw it again.

I packed up a bag right then and went to find the moment and Molly, but I haven't found either. I found the department Molly worked for, though. They remembered her, but they said she'd quit ten years ago and they didn't know where she was.

I got a job with the department and now I capture moments wherever I can. When I've got them alone, I ask them about Molly and

THE MOMENT

about the moment we shared together, but they never talk. It doesn't matter what I do to them.

Bernie

Billy decked this guy in the coffee shop around the corner from his place. Billy was at a table drinking a latte. This guy walked in and Billy got up and went over to him and hit him.

The guy was big. He had thick shoulders and legs like oak trees. He had a long, jutting forehead and a mean look on his face. He wasn't doing anything, though. He came in and got in line to order a drink and that was it.

Billy went right up to him and drilled him dead in the face. Billy was short when we were kids and he's still short. He was right up on his tiptoes to get the guy in the face. The guy reeled and Billy followed up. Billy got the jaw with the second shot and the guy dropped like a sack of wet rice.

Billy looked down and smiled. He realized the guy didn't recognize him. Billy took a second over that and then he got the hell out of there in case somebody else did and decided to call the cops. He told me about it over lunch.

"You remember Bernie Macintyre?" he said

Bernie'd picked on Billy from the time we were six until we were fourteen. After that Bernie moved. He stayed in the city, but he went to a different high school from Billie and me.

I hung out with Bernie once or twice. I wasn't tough, but I was the only kid in the class taller than Bernie and that was something. Bernie wasn't a bad guy, except for the way he picked on Billy.

"I decked the fucker. I decked him good," Billy said.

"How do you know it was him? It's been twenty years."

"I recognized him right off. I'll never forget that face."

"Did he recognize you?"

"I don't think so. It's kind of sad, but it's probably for the best. Assault charges and all that."

The next day, I saw a guy walking down the street in our neighbourhood. He was a big guy, bigger than me. He had a long, jutting forehead and a black eye and a purple jaw and a mean look on his face. I stared at him.

"You got a problem?" the guy said. "I'll send you to meet the other guy."

I held up my hands and kept walking. I'm not small, but I'm not tough. Somebody Billy's size, it took guts even to blindside a guy like that.

The guy wasn't Bernie, though. He looked a little bit like him, but he wasn't. Bernie always had sad eyes. They softened his face. Even most of the kids he picked on couldn't hate him.

This guy didn't have sad eyes. Everything about him was harsh. There's no sense telling Billy. He'll pretend he doesn't believe me, but secretly he'll feel bad that he decked some stranger and he shouldn't. One look at the guy and I can tell he had it coming from somewhere.

The Girl Next Door

At the wedding, a friend of mine told me being married would change my relationship with Pam. I don't know. Maybe it will, but so far it hasn't.

What has changed is my relationship with other women. I used to be nervous around other women. I was worried when I talked to them that maybe they'd think I was interested, even though I lived with my girlfriend. I was worried they'd get the wrong impression. They'd think I wanted to kiss them and eat them out and fuck them in the bathroom at Starbucks. Of course, I didn't want any of those things. Now I have a ring on my left hand and everyone can tell that I'm not interested in stuff like that.

Like the woman who's staying next door for a week. She went to high school with the neighbours or something. She was coming back from somewhere and we started talking.

She's pretty, this woman. She has long, dark hair and she's poured into her jeans. When I saw her I admired her and she noticed. While we talked, I rested my left hand on my right arm so she couldn't miss the ring.

If it had been a week ago, she might have thought I was checking her out, and then she might have thought that some of what I said was flirting. I would have been nervous about her getting the wrong impression. Now it's fine, though.

That's why I could invite her in, even though Pam was out with her maid of honour and she'd be out late because her maid of honour had to fly back to Vancouver the next day and they only see each other once or twice a year. Without a ring it wouldn't have been safe to invite a strange woman into the house.

With the ring on, though, I was relaxed and I was able to offer her a glass of wine, and to touch her cheek. We were able to stand in the kitchen and I was able to give her a kiss and there was no chance of misunderstanding.

It was the same when she grabbed her wine and my belt and led me to the bedroom. The layout of our house is completely different from the neighbours', so I don't know how she found the bedroom so easily, but it doesn't matter.

It was fine as we got undressed and lay down on the bed together and it was fine when she saw my hard-on.

If I hadn't had that ring on my left hand, she might have mistaken it all. She might have thought that I was interested in her as more than just a friend. She might have thought that I wanted to finger her and eat her pussy and fuck her, but I had my ring on. She knew I wasn't interested. She knew I wouldn't let anything happen. That's why she didn't object when I touched her breast, and it's why I wasn't concerned when she took my penis in her mouth.

Without the ring, it would all have been open to misinterpretation and something might have happened that I didn't want to happen.

Right in the Middle of Something

His entire life, Rob came in halfway through things. It wasn't just that he was never on time. He never missed things entirely, either. When Rob was born, the nurse had to catch him because the doctor was in the middle of an argument with his dad over whether or not there really were fifty-seven varieties of Heinz.

No one could remember Rob being on time for anything. Even Rob. He tried. Once in grade seven he set eighteen alarm clocks in an effort to be on time for school. By the time he figured out how to shut off all eighteen clocks, he was late. He got to school midway through a math test.

He once got to a ten o'clock meeting at ten o'clock. He was excited as hell, because he thought maybe things were changing. Then he walked into the room and found out the meeting had been moved up to nine-thirty.

He couldn't even go for coffee without coming in halfway through something. He had never once had a server stand there and smile and say, "Can I help you?" the way they did with other people. When Rob showed up they were mopping up spills and trying to fix espresso machines and fighting with customers. Once, a server was on the phone with her boyfriend and her boyfriend was breaking up with her.

People didn't like Rob. People who knew him a little thought he was disorganised or inconsiderate or both. People who didn't know him thought he hovered and eavesdropped. None of them realized how hard it was for Rob to come in halfway through stuff all the time. He missed the thread of narratives. He showed up places with no idea what was going on or what was being said. He knew people didn't like him, so he tried to piece together what he'd missed instead of asking them about it. At first there were a lot of misunderstandings, but Rob had gotten pretty good at figuring out the twists and turns of events.

There was only one person who put up with Rob: Ali. Ali had known Rob since they were little and he'd never seen Rob show up anytime but in the middle of things. He figured it had to be a curse, or maybe some sort of bizarre condition. Nobody could come in halfway through every single time unless they were cursed or had some sort of bizarre condition that made it that way. It was statistically so unlikely as to be effectively impossible.

Employers and doctors didn't agree with Ali. Rob went through a lot of jobs. They were all low paying, low end jobs where showing up late to the interview was better than not showing up at all.

That was Rob's life and it was lonely, especially since Ali had gotten married. Ali's wife thought the same things about Rob as everybody else.

Somehow, though, Rob met a woman. Her name was Laura. She was on the phone with her mom, arguing over whether or not she visited enough. She walked right into Rob. She dropped her phone and the battery popped out.

"Thank god," she said.

"Oh?"

"No, it's nothing. It's just my mom. She can be frustrating sometimes, you know? She insists on having these arguments that go nowhere."

"Will you have dinner with me? We could go somewhere nice and not argue. We could have a relaxing conversation and maybe it can go somewhere."

"Okay," she said.

They agreed on the next night at eight at a restaurant downtown. Rob was determined to be on time. He called Ali who was in the middle of chopping green onions and talking with his wife about having kids.

"How does he know?" Ali's wife said.

"I told you. It's a condition." Ali reached for his phone.

"Don't."

"Hello?"

"Ali. I've got a date. Tomorrow night at eight."

"Good for you buddy. That's awesome Rob."

"I need your help. I need to get there on time."

"I'll do what I can. I'll come by your place at seven. That should be plenty of time to get you there."

Ali showed up at Rob's at seven on the dot and Rob wasn't there. He was already at the restaurant. Rob had never wanted to be somewhere at the start of something so badly in his entire life. There was no way he was going to be late for this dinner. He went inside and walked up to the Hostess' podium. He was going to stand there and not move for an hour until his table was ready. If he just stood there and waited, he couldn't be late.

When Rob got to the podium there was a gunshot in the restaurant. Everybody ducked except Rob. He just stood there. A guy with a gun came up to Rob and put it in his face.

"Let's go outside," he said.

"I can't. I'm meeting someone," Rob said.

"Outside now, or I shoot you."

Rob tried to size the guy up. He had no context, so he had to guess. The guy sounded like he was prepared to shoot, but Rob couldn't say for sure. The only thing Rob knew was that if he went out that door, he'd be late meeting Laura.

"I can't. I'm sorry," Rob said.

"Get the fuck going," the guy said.

He punched Rob in the mouth with the gun and shoved him towards the door. Rob pushed back and the gun fired into Rob's face.

Laura got to the restaurant at eight. There were police and paramedics and tape, but Rob wasn't there. Around quarter after eight Ali showed up out of breath.

"Are you Laura?" he said.

"Yes. Who are you?"

"I'm a friend of Rob's. He's running a little late. He asked me to come by and let you know."

"Why didn't he just call me?"

"Apparently he lost his phone this morning."

RIGHT IN THE MIDDLE OF SOMETHING

Ali waited with Laura until quarter to nine.

"I'm sorry. I'm going," she said.

"No, no. He'll be here. I promise," Ali said.

"Too bad."

Ali hung around until nine-thirty and then he went home. Laura was pissed, but she'd been stood up before. Rob was just another asshole.

Ali found out about Rob the next day when the police called him to identify the body. When he saw the body and found out what time he'd been shot, Ali was pissed, because Rob had been on time. He'd even been early, which meant it wasn't a curse or some bizarre condition. It meant that Rob really had been the inconsiderate, disorganised asshole everyone else thought he was.

Murphy

Me and Joe and Mel got stuck in traffic when we were late for a meeting with a client. I was driving and Mel was beside me. Joe was in the back.

"Fuck. We're screwed," Joe said.

"Stupid Murphy's Law," Mel said.

"We should repeal Murphy's Law," I said.

We were over an hour late for the meeting and we lost the client. Behind his back Mel and I blamed it on Joe. Joe was our friend, but he was a goof off and management wanted to fire somebody.

Joe blamed the whole thing on Murphy's Law. "We were only a couple of minutes late and then we hit traffic." Joe got fired.

Joe hired a lawyer. He contested the firing and challenged the constitutionality of Murphy's Law. He called me up to tell me.

"I'm gonna get it repealed," he said. "I'll be a fucking hero man."

I figured the case would fizzle out, but the Supreme Court agreed to hear it. They even suspended Murphy's Law until the case could be heard.

There were ten months between the suspension of Murphy's Law and the close of hearings. Those ten months were a golden age for Canada. Only people who were early got caught in traffic. Weddings didn't get rained on. All kinds of things that could have gone wrong didn't.

Crime rates dropped drastically during those ten months. Instead of piling on, the little things made life better. News channels outside of Canada picked up the story and tourism exploded. Airlines had to cancel flights to all sorts of destinations in order to free up planes to send people to Canada. People came by the millions, but they all managed to time things perfectly. Planes didn't get held up. Visitors all found places to stay at great deals, but the hotel industry still made a killing.

When the case was finally called, it attracted huge international attention. Ottawa's population tripled to over three million people for the duration of the hearings. They packed the hotels and camped out in parks. They swarmed the courthouse and the courthouse lawn and Wellington Street. Police had no choice but to close the area off to traffic, and yet everything ran smoothly. Even the buses were on time, unless you were sprinting to catch one in which case it was miraculously waiting.

The trial lasted two weeks. It was shown on bar TVs across the country and on two huge screens on the courthouse lawn. It was the top story around the world too. Canada was a test case for the rest of the world. The first country to jettison Murphy's Law. Then the judges decided nine to nothing to keep it.

They ruled that the law applied equally to everyone so it was fair. They said that parliament could repeal the law, but so far not a single member has come forward to suggest it.

MURPHY

"Canada was a pretty good place before all this, and it continues to be a pretty good place," the leader of the opposition said. "I don't want to interfere in something that might be a provincial matter," the prime minister said, and the premiers said that it wasn't a good time what with the economy and all.

I figure the real reason is Murphy's Law itself. If whatever can go wrong will, something must have gone wrong for them all to have gotten elected.

In the next election there'll be a whole bunch of candidates vowing to chuck Murphy's Law, though. Somebody's already registered a party called the Murphyites and they have no shortage of candidates.

I wish the Murphyites well. Why not? But even if they win the law won't get repealed. Something will go wrong.

My Reputation

My reputation started preceding me in my early twenties. I'd show up at a party and there he'd be in the corner by the lamp. My reputation was a short, skinny, little guy with a beard and a mixed drink. I don't think I ever saw him with a beer or a glass of wine.

He was always talking to someone, usually a woman. He was a lecherous fuck. He'd lean drunkenly against the wall and paw at the women. He was already drunk when I'd show up and he'd leave fifteen minutes after I got there.

It took me a long time to realize that that was who he was. At first I didn't pay much attention to him. He was just some guy at a party, and I never talked to him. But he was at every party, and then I started seeing him other places. I'd go out to dinner and he'd be paying his bill. I'd go for a coffee and he'd be four places ahead of me in line.

It was odd, because I didn't know him. In fact, no one I knew, knew him either. I asked around. Nobody seemed to know who he was.

One night at a party I asked a woman he'd been talking to. "I don't know. Just some guy. I've seen him around. I think he was drunk," she said. Then she asked me if my name was Steve.

"Yeah, how did you know?"

"I've seen you around," she said and walked away.

People began to recognize me everywhere I went. Complete strangers. They nodded at me and winked at me and said, "Hey Steve." Sometimes they crossed the street and I had the feeling they were trying to avoid me.

I was out at dinner and a guy came up to my table. "You're Steve, aren't you," he said. "I'm Larry. It's nice to finally meet you. I've heard a lot about you."

"All good I hope," I said and he gave me an odd look.

I decided to ask around and see what was being said about me. It turned out there was a lot being said about me, and most of it was really scurrilous shit.

My reputation had me divorced twice with another marriage on the rocks and four kids, one of whom belonged to a twenty year old stripper. My reputation also had me doing five years for fraud and snorting coke off of hookers. I was a baseball prospect who'd blown out his knee and worked nights as a janitor at an elementary school. I was an alcoholic, who was in and out of rehab and I'd killed a guy in Ireland when I was a student.

It wasn't until I was thirty-eight that I finally put together where all of this was coming from. I was at a club downtown and a woman came up and introduced herself.

"I'm Ellen," she said. She was tall and pretty and elegant.

"I'm ..."

"You are Stephen Golding. Your reputation precedes you," she said.

MY REPUTATION

That's when I figured out that the guy was my reputation. He was everywhere I was before I was and he always cleared out when I got there. It had to be him.

"Oh yeah? What does my reputation say?"

"It varies," she said.

We danced and I asked her to come back to my place.

"I'd like to. How much of what they say is true?" she said.

"Some. Not much."

We danced some more, but I went home alone.

I decided to talk to my reputation, but he was a slippery fucker. He'd be in his corner when I'd come in and catching him would look simple, but he'd find a way out. He caught on that I was after him and he took to hanging out near the exits. Whenever I'd show up at a place he'd bolt. Somehow he seemed to know which door I'd come through and hang out by a different one.

He put it about that I was after him. A misunderstanding, he said, and then he said I wasn't known for my understanding. The last guy to try and explain, he said.

It took months of trying, but I cornered him. It was at a cocktail party hosted by a woman from work. My reputation got himself caught in the middle of the hall, too far from the door and I forced him up the stairs. He ran into the bathroom and locked the door. I figured I had him, but he managed to get out the window and down to the ground. It took the woman who owned the house an hour to get the bathroom door open.

It was another three months before I caught him. We were in a Starbucks. I didn't see him until I was already at the cash. He ran and I

201

went after him. It cost me a twenty and I didn't get my coffee, but I caught him. My reputation wasn't in very good shape.

He turned down a side street and I was right on him. I tripped him and then I kicked him in the gut.

"Stop putting my name about," I said and he smirked. "You think it's funny, you little fucker? All this bullshit about me you're going around telling everybody. Do you have any idea what you're doing to my reputation and you don't even know me?"

"I am your reputation," he said.

"It seems like it, but not anymore." I bent over and punched him a few times. "You put about any more lies about me and I'll fucking kill you."

"Whatever happened to 'just so long as you get my name right'?" he said and I punched him some more. "I'm just trying to help you man. You're lucky. At least you've got a reputation. Most people, nobody knows about them one way or the other."

I punched him again. I reached into his pocket for his wallet, but he didn't have one. Just sixty-two dollars and a debit card with my name on it. I shoved the debit card in my pocket. I held up the money. "I guess this must be mine too," I said and shoved it in my pocket.

Then I grabbed him by the collar and punched him some more. "I was serious. I better not see you again."

"I'm sorry man. I was just doing my job," he said. I knocked his head on the pavement and he passed out. I dragged him to the side of the road and left him. That was the last I saw of him for three years.

Things were different without my reputation around. I'd go places and nobody'd know who I was. At functions and parties people would ask about me. I'd show up and they'd whisper and ask if anyone knew me.

As time went by it got more extreme. People I'd worked with and been friends with for years complained they didn't know me anymore. I stopped getting invited places. I'd stop for coffee and people would look at me funny, like I didn't belong.

Eventually, even people I knew stopped recognizing me. One day I showed up for work and security escorted me out of the building. That's when I started looking for my reputation. He wasn't easy to track down. He wasn't on Facebook or Twitter. I tried Google and I tried online high school yearbooks, but there was nothing. I asked around with people I used to know, but nobody had any idea about him.

After two months I hired a private detective. He did a composite sketch and asked around, but he didn't have any luck either. After six months my old job figured out that I wasn't working there anymore and my paycheques stopped.

I kept the detective on anyway. He ran through most of my savings, but he tracked down my reputation. He was in Vancouver. He'd taken on a proper identity. He had a job and money and a girlfriend.

I packed a bag and went to Vancouver. I hitchhiked to save money. It took me two weeks. I camped out in front of the building where he worked and when he came out I walked beside him. He'd shaved the beard, but otherwise he looked the same. When he saw me he smiled.

"You want to go for a drink?" he said.

We went to a sports bar around the corner and he ordered a mixed drink.

"I need you back," I said.

"Sorry man."

"I'll make it worth your while."

"Sure. You know, it was an interesting time, but I'm not going back. I've got a name and a life of my own now. It's kind of daunting at first, but you get used to it."

"Listen you little shit. You're my reputation. That means you belong to me," I said.

"I was your reputation. You fired me, remember."

"Look, I'm desperate man. I didn't realize. I didn't appreciate. I'm sorry man."

"I can't help you," he said. He wrote a name and address on a piece of paper. "This guy might be able to."

"Who is he?"

"He's the one who hired me. He's based out here."

I looked the guy up. His place was on the lower east side. It was a three-storey walk-up. It looked like it hadn't had a coat of paint in forty years. I banged on the door anyway. This guy let me in and sat me on a couch covered in cat hair.

"What can I do for you?"

"I need a new reputation," I said.

"Oh, hey, you're the one who fired my man."

"I'm sorry. I didn't know."

"Of course not. You can't just let a thing like that out. If people knew, there'd be an investigation and then I'd either get shut down or have to pay taxes or something. At any rate, I can't give you a new reputation."

"I can't keep going on like this."

"I understand. I'd even like to help you out, but I've got a shortage of applicants at the moment. Now, if you wanted a job, I could arrange that."

"No thanks."

"Well, I sell crack too. Without a reputation you should either take the job or the crack."

I took the job. I got set up with some guy in Chicago. It's not so bad. Chicago's a big city, so nobody thinks too much about some stranger. There are times when it's crushing, not being my own person. Those are the times I really rubbish the guy.

Before I started, they gave me a file on him, but I haven't bothered to read it. Besides, it's like they say: "as long as you get the name right."

Good Riddance Matthew Goldman

Matthew Goldman died. He was a hundred-and-sixteen. That made him the second oldest person alive. Grace Cole is a hundred-and-nineteen. Matthew Goldman's special, though, because he was the last unrecorded human.

Grace grew up in New York City and her father was a technofile so we have a complete record of her right from birth. Not Matthew Goldman. He grew up on a farm in Iowa. His father was a crazy old bastard in his sixties who forbade computers and video cameras from the property. We actually know very little of Matthew's first fifteen years. That's when satellite cameras reached a level of technology that allowed us to observe what was happening at every point in the world.

With Matthew dead it's the end of an era. Finally, after five thousand years. Most people didn't even know who Matthew Goldman was. His obituary is all over the net now, but before that. Matthew was frustrating for us. Fifteen years is a lot of missing data. We never really knew who Matthew Goldman was.

With his death, Matthew's story has picked up a cult following. Mostly it's so-called historians and disgruntled twenty-somethings. My son's friend Harry is the hero of the movement.

Harry was the last person to interview Matthew Goldman. He was also the last person to ask him about being unrecorded. The rest of Matthew's life was taken up with talking about bridge and who was dying at the home where he lived.

The interview is interesting. Matthew talks about "the way the world used to be and the way it has gone." "I really regret that," he said. It seems he genuinely believed that the world was a better place when we didn't know everything about everybody. He couldn't seem to grasp how much more reliable the world is now.

He also said, "it's important to remember that recording devices still can't tell what you're thinking. All this talk about brainwaves being monitored and shit. I probably won't live to see the day, but if nobody takes a stand, you will." He said it like brainwave monitoring was a bad thing. Then he went on to say, "Guard your thoughts. They're the only things you've still got that are private. Nobody knows what you're thinking."

Harry actually believes this. My son does too, although he won't say it in front of me. He puts forward this garbage about how brainwaves should only be monitored by governments and he's worried about the private corporate interests who will be in charge of collecting and translating them.

Right now it doesn't look good for their movement. Government and the majority of academic opinion are onside with the program. They understand that Matthew Goldman was wrong. It used to be true that you couldn't know what someone was thinking, but it's not anymore. That died with Matthew Goldman.

GOOD RIDDANCE MATTHEW GOLDMAN

We have a complete record of everybody and we can tell what they're thinking. Expressions give it all away. The myth of the poker face has been widely dispelled. If we've seen every expression that a person has ever made and the situations that they've made them in, then we can predict their reactions. Research bears this out. That's why there's so little crime these days.

There is still crime, though. Even with computers monitoring the world and monitoring the archives of different people, and millions of people monitoring the computers, we can't catch everything. It takes too long to cross-reference it all. Monitoring brainwaves will dramatically speed up this process.

I can understand where the resistance comes from. People consistently resist change. It's not widely known, but Matthew Goldman was a historian. Harry's father was too. There are still a few people out there who claim to be modern historians and there are a number of ancient historians around. It's too much for these people to admit that the past is no longer relevant. The purpose of studying history is to help us understand our present, but we know everything about our present through simple observation. The historians have a vested interest though. Their jobs are in danger, and admitting the irrelevance of the past means admitting that their lives are pointless.

And so they cling to the notion that you can't tell what people are thinking, because if you can tell what they're thinking and you have a complete data record, then there's no need to write about anything. Historians claim to provide nuance, but we know everything. Nuance is obsolete.

Harry's interview is being watched, though, and people seem to be sympathetic. If it gains enough traction, it could set society back hundreds of years.

It hasn't reached that point yet and fortunately we'll know that it's going to before it does and we should be able to stop it. For now, these people can mourn the death of Matthew Goldman all they want. It's the end of an era, but era's end. Uncertainty makes life difficult. Without Matthew Goldman, there is no uncertainty.

People have sought knowledge for millennia. Now that we have it people gripe. That's natural, but it's wrong. History is over and we need to move on. Good riddance Matthew Goldman.

My Neighbour's Dog

When I was twelve, my neighbour's dog went missing. It must have been hard for my neighbour, because it was just the two of them. The morning after it happened, my friend Joey came up to me in the school yard and said: "Did you hear your neighbour's dog ran away?" I'd heard, but it was ridiculous to say she'd run away because she was older than we were and she had bad arthritis.

Everyone in the neighbourhood knew my neighbour and his dog. Especially the kids. My neighbour and his dog lived four doors down from the school. She sat on the front lawn all day and when we walked by she got up and barked at us.

The dog was named Muddle. My neighbour told me she got her name because he found her lying in a mud puddle looking confused. She was about twelve weeks old then.

My neighbour said Muddle was a Heinz fifty-seven. He said he'd asked the vet what kind of dog her parents might have been and the vet had said: "Your guess is as good as mine." She was shaggy everywhere except her face and her fur was mostly brown, but it was also black and white in patches. She was bigger than my friend Joey's beagle, but she was smaller than my cousin Tom's Labrador. My parents wouldn't let me get a dog.

Sometimes my neighbour stood on the lawn with Muddle because he was retired and it was just the two of them. When he was out, they'd both come over to the curb and she'd sniff the kids between barks and he'd ask us about our days.

He'd always ask me if I'd gotten into a fight. Most days I hadn't. There were always fights in the schoolyard. Once in a while I got into fights, but not usually. I think he figured I didn't fight enough.

My neighbour and his dog were a little weird but mostly I liked them. At Halloween they always gave out unshelled peanuts, which was what I liked least about them back then. My neighbour sometimes made comments about the Blacks and the Jews and the Chinese, but almost everybody at our school was white and I didn't think about it. When I grew up, that bothered me more than the unshelled peanuts and mostly I avoided my neighbour like the rest of the adults did.

It didn't used to be just my neighbour and his dog. He'd had a wife and five kids, but the kids were grown up and the wife was gone. He talked a lot about his kids, but I don't remember them ever visiting.

My mom said that his wife was "long suffering" and that once the kids were gone, she divorced him. My dad said it was true but nevertheless you shouldn't gossip.

The September I was twelve my neighbour rang our doorbell. I had just started grade seven, which meant I went to a different school and didn't walk by his house anymore. I answered the door.

"Oh, hi Jim. I was just wondering if you'd seen Muddle," my neighbour said.

"I haven't seen her."

"Okay. Thanks. If you see her can you let me know?"

He looked really sad so I said, "Sure," and then I said, "I can help you look if you want."

MY NEIGHBOUR'S DOG

"Can you?"

"Sure. I just need shoes."

I put on my running shoes and went outside. My neighbour and I split up. He kept going up the street and I went to the schoolyard and then to the park. Nobody'd seen Muddle and eventually I gave up and went home.

I was late for dinner. My plate was sitting on the kitchen table with a pot lid over it.

"It's cold by now," my mom said. "You didn't tell me where you were going."

"Muddle went missing," I said. "I went to look for her."

"You should have told me where you were going."

Dinner was fish sticks and peas. I didn't like them when they were hot, but they were worse cold.

Muddle didn't come home that day or the next. Joey said we should do up flyers on his computer. We told my neighbour and he told us to say there was a reward for her return, so we wrote that on the flyers. We taped the flyers on lamp posts around the neighbourhood and shoved them in the faces of people we saw.

Muddle didn't show up. After a month, everybody figured that Muddle was dead, but the posters stayed up, except for the one that we'd put up at McDonald's that the manager took down.

In October, I was riding my bike home from school. It was really warm out for October and I was wearing a t-shirt and shorts. I went down the hill and across the bus road. There was a bridge going over the road and it was just as fast to go that way, but it was illegal to cross the road.

On the other side of the road, there was a small forest. There was a narrow dirt path through the trees that led down to a creek that was shallow enough to ride your bike through. I stopped when I got to the edge of the creek. It was a nice, quiet place and I liked being there. I took off my socks and shoes and walked out into the creek. The creek bed was rocky and slippery and I fell on my ass.

I heard a bark and looked up to see Muddle splashing through the water towards me. She wasn't very far away. She covered half the distance to me in four steps and stopped to take a drink. Her fur was wet and matted and she was so skinny I could see her ribs. She barked again and I stuck out my hand and she came over to me. She sniffed my hand and licked it. Her breath stank. After a minute or so, she limped off down the creek in the same direction she'd been going.

I went back to the shore, put on my socks and shoes and biked home. I didn't tell my neighbour, or my parents or Joey. I never told anyone, and Muddle never came home. And then today, I was at my parents' after work.

My mom had lent me a book by some local author that she said I absolutely had to read. I'd had the book for six months and I hadn't read it. I gave it to her and told her I hadn't read it.

"You can hang onto it a bit longer if you want," she said.

"I'm not going to read it," I said.

The neighbour's house was for sale and I mentioned it.

"He died about a week ago," my mom said. "His children didn't waste much time."

When I got home, my wife was making dinner. I went into the kitchen and stood there watching her.

MY NEIGHBOUR'S DOG

"You could make yourself useful," she said.

I took a knife from the block and an onion from the fridge and started chopping. I told my wife about my neighbour and Muddle and how I'd seen Muddle later on and hadn't done anything.

"I've never told anybody about seeing Muddle," I said when I was done.

"I don't understand. How could you just do nothing? You didn't even tell your neighbour?" she said. I shrugged. "That's too much onion," she said and after that she didn't talk to me for the rest of the night.

The Average Price of a Cup of Coffee in Seattle

Martin crunched the numbers and it turned out humanity's books didn't balance. He added up everything everybody had and subtracted everything everybody owed. It turned out humanity was in for trillions.

It took Martin sixty years to figure out the books. He kept having to start over at the beginning because it took too long to gather the data. It wasn't until recently, thanks to technology, that he was able to complete his project. He was eighty-six when he finally finished.

It's hard to imagine it was worth it. Martin spent his life broke and alone and when he finally completed his accounting, experts denounced him like the church denounced Galileo. Economists and financiers everywhere claimed that Martin's methods were questionable and that his conclusion was just plain wrong.

Martin defended himself in interviews on the BBC, CNN, MSNBC, even Fox. He went on and he calmly explained why he was right. Then the cops found him beaten to death in a hotel room in New York City.

After Martin died, a couple of MIT students decided to check his work. It took them a night to compile the data and four months to process it. They came to the same conclusion as Martin.

"Unless the average citizen of Jibouti has a net worth of approximately one hundred and ninety billion dollars, then the world's books don't balance," they wrote in their report.

Wall Street firms still claimed this was impossible, but economists started to look seriously at the problem. They did their own studies that came to the same conclusions as Martin and the MIT students.

Once the economists started saying it, the world panicked. People called for a general cancellation of debts. It didn't happen, because some very important people made a lot of money on the interest off what they'd loaned, and after all they'd loaned it in good faith.

Wall Street came up with a plan to solve the problem. They created a debt retirement fund and speculated on it. It raked in tons of money. The shares rose dramatically in price. After six months, the fund had brought humanity's net worth to within the cost of an average priced cup of coffee in Seattle of zero. Then it stayed there. No matter what anybody did, they couldn't get rid of that last cup of coffee.

There were all kinds of theories, but no human could solve it. That's where I come in. I was contracted as an independent auditor. My job is to check all of humanity's books individually. The argument goes that previous accountings may have missed things that aren't part of the global network. Every account on Earth has been frozen until the completion of my report.

THE AVERAGE PRICE OF A CUP OF COFFEE

Obviously I've had to do all the work myself. There's too much opportunity for graft to trust a job like this to a team of people.

People will try to buy you off over all kinds of things. They don't want their neighbours to know that they've got a toaster. They're worried about getting caught stealing rice from the packaging plant, or that the government will find out they're working full-time while drawing welfare. But the worst are the governments themselves. There's all kinds of stuff they don't want getting out.

I've been through the whole process three times now, and each time humanity comes up short by exactly the cost of an average priced cup of coffee in Seattle.

Humanity's not happy about it, but the interplanetary community is quite excited. What it means is that the Earth's credit rating will be reduced to junk status.

Somebody will step in to cover the debt. The corporation that my brother works for is seriously considering it. They know humanity will have to default on the loan and then they can foreclose on the Earth.

I feel bad for humanity, because it turns out that it all has to do with some alien in the nineties who found himself in Seattle. He ordered a coffee that cost what the average cup of coffee in Seattle costs and then he skipped out without paying.

The Success Audit

They audited the Department of Success because of Theresa Haig. The Department of Success is my department. I've been the director for a hundred and six years.

The rumour is that the audit isn't good. The rumour is that the audit is going to say the department is a mess and nobody knows what's going on. The rumour is that the audit will recommend I be fired, and the rumour is that I will be fired.

It's not how I wanted it to end. My predecessor retired after three hundred and twelve years and they gave his nepotistic ass an award for outstanding service.

It's true that the department is a mess. We're working on it, but I feel like I've done a lot. I've tried to reduce discrimination and make success a meritocracy. It hasn't been easy. There's a lot of pressure from certain quarters to maintain the status quo. People don't quit on their families and friends just because they're dead.

The rumour is that that's not what the audit is going to say, though. The rumour is that the audit's going to say that nineteen percent of people destined for success don't achieve it and that another thirty-eight percent are less successful than they're supposed to be.

It goes the other way too. People who are supposed to fail are ending up rich and famous. That violates the idea of ordination. Rumour has it that "If anyone can succeed or fail regardless of preordination, then what purpose do the Department of Success and the Department of Failure serve?" will be in the audit.

Otherwise the Department of Failure will get off scot-free. It was beyond the scope of the audit, like the two departments aren't interconnected.

The audit's been coming for a while. To be honest I'm surprised they didn't do it twenty years ago. Running the Department of Success is getting complicated. It really got started in the sixties when they introduced a Success Ombudsman in response to a series of plane crashes that killed famous people. As if famous people somehow had a right to grieve premature death that the rest of us didn't.

Buddy Holly was the worst of them. He nearly brought down the department in his bitterness. I spent years negotiating with him through the ombudsman. I hate that ombudsman. I can never figure out whether he has it in for me or for the entire department. It looks like he's at least got me now.

Theresa Haig was the one that did me in. She was destined for success. Her biography was set up like the really great successes that come out of nowhere. Her neighbours, her teachers, the kids she went to school with, they all knew she was going to be a success. She knew it too. Nobody could ever figure out what she was going to be successful at, though. That's because her file, which would have told us and allowed us to set her on the appropriate path, got misplaced.

Nobody much would have noticed, but Theresa was an only child and she had those kinds of parents. Theresa's parents, Eddie and Lily set her up for success. They were both frustrated, middling talents. She worked in the civil service and he sold diamonds. Any money they had went towards making sure Theresa was a success.

When Theresa turned forty and she still wasn't a success, Lily, who was dead by then, got in touch with a friend of her father's who worked in the Department of Success. He hunted around, but he couldn't find Theresa's file. He told Lily that. He also told Lily that he'd remembered seeing her file and that she was supposed to be "big".

Lily let it drop until Theresa died in a car crash a year later. Then she freaked out. She could have gone after the Department of Mortality. So could Buddy Holly. Our job isn't to make sure that successes don't die, it's to make sure they're successes. But then figuring out what goes on at the Department of Mortality is almost impossible and they don't have an ombudsman.

When Theresa died, her mom went straight to the success ombudsman. Arguably the case was outside his mandate. Theresa wasn't a success and she didn't bring the complaint herself. It didn't matter. The ombudsman got involved. Of course we stonewalled him. You don't just let a guy like that go through your files. He called for an audit and they gave it to him.

As part of my efforts to reform the Department of Success and reduce nepotism, I've tried to close the department to anyone who can still trace themselves to the living. I've managed to reduce the numbers of these people, but the policy has been declared discriminatory. If I'd been allowed to implement the policy, the audit might never have happened.

The rumour is that the audit has nothing to say on that either, though. In fact the rumour is that rather than accusing the leak of acting inappropriately in doing a favour for a friend of the family, the audit will praise him as "a courageous whistleblower."

The only consolation is that the audit won't say anything about how her file got lost. Nobody but me knows that it sat in the bottom drawer of the desk in my office at home for twenty-four years before it turned up in the basement at the Department of Failure.

In a hundred and six years I've been interested in several successful people, but they won't have anything to do with me. Even when they're dead the successful all stick together. It's sick.

Of all of them, Theresa was the greatest. I've had a crush on her since she was a teenager. If she'd succeeded like the others, she never would have had anything to do with me.

For a normal person, though, I'm a good catch. Head of one of the largest departments in the afterlife. At least until Monday when the audit comes out.

Soul Mate

My wife and I weren't soul mates. Sometimes people thought we were, but we weren't. I never thought about it much, because I didn't really believe in soul mates, but they exist.

When you die, if your soul mate is already dead, then you get put together and off you go. If you die before your soul mate, you hang out with the others whose soul mates are still alive.

My wife and I were married for fifty-four years. The last few years, I was kind of sick of her, but then she died and I missed her all the time. When I died and there I was, just a soul, I was excited to see her. Then I found out that she was already with her soul mate.

"It happens all the time," one woman told me. "I outlived four husbands and not one was my soul mate. Most of us don't end up married to our soul mates. It seems to happen once every couple of generations that somebody marries their soul mate. Most of us didn't even know our soul mates while we were alive."

There wasn't much I could do, so I followed the crowd. I hung out in the singles clubs and waited. The clubs of lonely souls some smartass called them.

It wasn't bad at first. We were all impatient for our soul mates, but we tried to pretend that we weren't. We killed time by drinking and fucking on couches in the clubs in front of all the other souls.

After the clubs closed at four, we went to the all night pizza parlours and it was fun.

It got dull though. With no body, there's no sensation and the longer you're away from your body, the less you can remember the feelings.

Most people aren't stuck in the clubs too long. A couple of years at the most. They try and time it so that soul mates die around the same time. When I died, Elise had been in the clubs the longest. She'd been dead nine years and she was still alone.

She was bored. She couldn't figure out what else to do, though, so she did the same things more. She fucked ten or twelve guys a night, often more than one at a time. She liked me and I liked her and we hung out a lot. We'd go out for pizza and she'd eat an entire extra-large with extra cheese. After she'd feel sick and have to lie down. I'd carry her back to her bed and she'd pass out.

I started to stay at her place. We'd hang out during the day. We'd go around and watch the couples and make faces at them.

Elise was alone for fourteen years in total. She was famous at the clubs for how long she'd been around. Then one day she disappeared. After her, there was only one guy who'd been there longer than me.

"Five years. Really? Usually they try to time it," one woman told me.

"How do you know?"

"It's what I've heard, but then, I haven't been here as long as you."

"Yeah, well, it's true. Sometimes it doesn't work out, though," I said.

But it worked out for everyone else. I stayed in the clubs as the years kept going. People pitied me because I'd been there so long. I became like Elise. I drank all night and I fucked constantly and I could eat more pizza than anyone.

Once I saw Elise walking down the street. I tried to talk to her, but it was awkward. She smiled at me while I talked, but she hung off her soul mate. She didn't care about me.

I decided to track down my wife. It took me four months, but I found her. It turned out her soul mate was a woman from rural China. The soul mate was in the room the entire time we talked.

"Til death do us part," my wife finally said and that was the end of it.

I figured if there was an afterlife, somebody had to be responsible for coordinating it, so I went in search of the administration. I'd never seen an office, but there had to be one somewhere. I asked around, but nobody seemed to know. Part of the problem was that the souls who had been paired up didn't like to associate with the ones who hadn't. The single souls hung out in the clubs and pizza parlours and the couples drifted around and didn't need anything else. They didn't even need other couples.

Nobody actually ran the clubs or pizza parlours. People got their own drinks and made their own pizzas. Death was a pathetic existence, but nobody seemed to notice. They were either with their partners or fucking and eating and waiting.

Except me. I'd been there so long without meeting my soul mate that I became a legend. It got so I forgot what it felt like to do things. I did them anyway though, because there was nothing else. Eventually the other souls started to avoid me. They figured something had to be wrong with me.

I got banned from the clubs and the pizza parlours. Sometimes I managed to sneak in to use the bathrooms. Going to the bathroom was the one habit I couldn't break. The rest of the time I lurked about outside. I'd corner souls on the street and beg them to fuck me or at least to get me a slice of pizza.

I got so desperate for contact of some kind that I forced one soul up against the side of Fida's Pizza and tried to make her have sex with me. Some other souls came along and pulled me away. It didn't matter. I couldn't feel anything anyway.

Sometimes I wandered away from the clubs, but it was worse outside the singles' district. The solitary souls actively ignored me, but the couples didn't even notice me. I finally stopped one couple. They looked at me angrily.

"Are you happy?" I said.

"Get out of our way," one of them said.

"That's not an answer. It's insane. Are you ever apart? I've never seen a couple apart. How can you be happy like that?"

They moved me aside and kept going about their business. I followed them around for an hour and it didn't bug them. They were in their own world. They went to a little stream in a meadow with wildflowers and just sat. They didn't picnic or frolic, they just sat.

"Ah, what the fuck?" I said and they ignored me.

When one of them finally stood up, I pushed him into the stream. I jumped on him and held him under the water. His partner went and joined him. They lay under the water together with me on top.

I went back to the clubs, because it was less depressing. I wandered the streets like before. Occasionally I managed to get into a place unnoticed. I used the bathroom and ate and drank what I could before somebody recognized me.

Usually, though, I had to wait outside. There were dumpsters behind the pizza parlours and sometimes people would throw food in them.

I met Edgar in the back alley behind Fida's Pizza. He was a shrivelled up, dirty soul. He surprised the hell out of me when he came out of the dumpster and grabbed a half-eaten leftover out of my hand.

"Hey, what the fuck?" I said.

"It's mine now," he said and he dove back into the dumpster.

I leaned over the lip of the dumpster and yanked him out.

"Who the fuck are you?" I said.

"Edgar."

"What are you doing back here all alone?"

"Same as you."

"Oh yeah. What's that?"

"Existing."

"How long have you been here?"

"Eternity. I don't really remember being alive. Barely. Little things. I've been here longer than the pizza parlours."

"Where's your partner?" I said.

"Soul mate," he said.

"Sure. Where's your soul mate?"

"There was an odd number in my generation. It happens sometimes. I think it's been awhile since it happened. It feels like it's been awhile."

"What are you saying? Are you saying I might not have a soul mate?"

"I'm saying you don't. Just because I live in a dumpster doesn't mean I don't know what's being said. You're on your own."

"So now what?"

"Exist," he said. He tried the back door of Fida's Pizza, but it was locked. "There used to be a guy came here a lot who took pity. He always unlocked the door when he ate here."

"So if we're both alone, why don't they pair us up?" I said.

"Fuck. Don't take this personally, but I don't want to spend eternity with you," he said.

I punched Edgar in the gut and picked him up and threw him back in the dumpster. Then I went and tried the back doors to some other places. I found a club that was open and I went into the back room and drank their entire stock of alcohol. Then I found a park bench and lay down until morning.

How it Ended

I'm twenty-seven and I'm dead. I had a heart attack. I'm not even overweight, and I bike everywhere, so what the hell?

Especially the way it ended. I was fifteen seconds from coming when I keeled over. I was fucking this woman doggy style and I was sort of getting a rhythm and then I just fell on her and she went splat into the mattress.

That's how it ended. The rest of it didn't go that differently. It seems a little unfair.

I almost died a virgin. At twenty-seven. Maybe I actually did die a virgin. Does it count if you don't come?

I wasn't saving myself. I didn't try to stay a virgin until twenty-seven. That's just how it happened.

The woman I was fucking was thirty-three. She was pretty and she had a good job. She owned her own house with a king-sized bed. She had everything together. We were on her king-sized bed and I was fucking her and thinking that things were turning around and I died.

I was just getting the hang of fucking her when I collapsed. They make it look so easy in porn movies, but it's hard to get it in the hole and it's hard to find the rhythm.

I was dead before she rolled me off. I hope she managed to roll me off all right. The bed was pretty soft. I feel bad for her. Something like that's got to be really shitty for the person who's still alive too.

It turns out there is a god. I would have bet ten to one against, but I opened my eyes and there he was.

"Welcome Marcus," he said. He was twice my size with this big white beard and an impeccably tailored suit.

"What the hell?" I said.

"I have summoned you to me. This is not hell," god said.

"Are you god?" I said.

"Yes," he said.

I lit into god. I mean I really tore him a new one. "Where do you get off?" "You've got some balls." "Go fuck yourself." That sort of thing.

God hit me in the chest with a bolt of lightning. It was very old testament. I called god a tin pot little dictator and he hit me with a second, larger lightning bolt right in the groin. The thunder from it's left me deaf.

God stood there while I lay on the ground. He pointed at me and it looked like he was laughing. Then he turned away. His shoulders shook. I think he was still laughing.

I walked up behind god and stuck a sign on his back. It said "free will," or "kick me." One of those.

Repeat

When I was six or seven my mom forgot me in the grocery store. She got the groceries loaded into the car, got home and got them unloaded before she noticed and came back for me. I was having fun playing on the rocket ship by the entrance. There was an old woman on the bench beside the rocket ship who kept giving me quarters for some reason. Then my mom showed up all panicked and crying so I cried too.

My mom told me how sorry she was, but I just balled. Finally she got fed up. She sighed and said, "look, if I could go back in time and change things, I would, but I can't and nobody else can either."

I assumed that was true, but it wasn't entirely. My mom didn't know, because she couldn't go back in time, but some people can. There aren't very many of them, but they exist. Nobody's got a number on them, but if they were all that common, regular people would figure it out. The ability to go back in time seems to be genetic, but it's recessive, so it doesn't really catch on.

My girlfriend can go back in time. Anytime she wants, she can just take a do-over. She admitted that she's already used it several times in our relationship. If she hadn't we might be broken up already. Now that I know, we'll probably have to break up soon.

I know because she told me. I was suspicious that something was going on and she could tell. She said nobody else had ever been suspicious and she told me the truth because she loves me. She explained the whole thing to me.

She said that people like her can just undo all the bad shit that happens to them whenever they want. She said she was in a skiing accident when she was nine and broke her right leg. She said kids can't do it, not until adolescence. It wasn't until she was thirty and developed arthritis in her right leg that she went back in time and told her dad that she didn't feel like skiing and now her leg's fine.

At first when she told me it seemed unfair. She said that the rest of us keep going on and our memories adjust to the changes that people like her make. Sometimes our minds use dreams to get rid of old memories, which is why dreams make no sense.

She's telling the truth about it. When she's gone, I'm hoping this will jog my memory, but it won't. Probably I'll just figure I was drunk and decided to try my hand at writing fiction. I didn't tell her I was going to write it down, but she seems to know. She even told me not to use her name.

Maybe I wrote about her once before and she came back to warn me not to but couldn't bring herself to, or maybe she just knows how I am. She said that it's not a new idea, that people have written stories about it before. It's just that people who can't go back refuse to accept that others can. People need to believe that they're the best the universe has.

I've had pangs of bitterness over it. My life's been okay, but there's shit I'd change if I could. When she told me how she could go back in time I got so angry that I almost hit her. It seemed so manipulative, just fixing your life. What about the other people who are affected? I forced myself to listen, though and she talked and I realized how fucked up the whole thing is.

For the people who can go back in time, it becomes a compulsion. My girlfriend said that things don't really get better each time. She said that after awhile it even seems all the same, but you keep going back anyway. She said that some of them try to get old, but they can't make it because they keep thinking about how it was better before. They have a couple of drinks and they get all sentimental about how they were young and beautiful and their bodies didn't ache and then they wake up and they're teenagers again.

The more I think about it, the more I feel sorry for my girlfriend. At night, I hold her and stroke her hair and I cry for her. I can tell she's getting tired of that. Nobody likes to be pitied, especially for being able to do something you can't. It won't be long now before this never happened.

Note: The author of this piece lives alone. He has never lived with a woman. And the preceding is entirely a work of fiction.

Acknowledgements

So as not to omit anyone: Thanks!

About the Author

Andrew J Simpson was born and raised in Ottawa and lives in Toronto. His stories have appeared in journals both in Canada and internationally. He was awarded the Nicholas Hoare Prize for Short Fiction in 2005. This is his first anthology.

For more information on what he is doing check out versustheneanderthals.com.

Also from
BareBackPress

The Cure for Consciousness
Peter Jelen

YOU HAVE A DISEASE.
YOUR BRAIN IS INFECTED.
POISONED.
CONTAMINATED.

But don't worry. Ernie Lobe, a fifty-four year old baker, sociopath, and father of two is looking for the cure, which he thinks he may have found. The only problem is there's a slight side-effect...death. But don't worry about that either, because you can get paid to die.

$12.99
132 Pages
6" x 9"
ISBN -13: 978-0988075061
BISAC: Fiction/ General

Unwrapped:
The BareBack Anthology

Unwrapped: The BareBack Anthology is a collection of innovative poetry from poets speckled around the world who have been featured in BareBack Magazine, an online publication dedicated to BareBack writers. People who aren't afraid to take off their gloves and give the world sincere, unpretentious, honest writing that has punch.

$17.99
136 Pages
6" x 9"
ISBN 13: 978-0988075047
BISAC: Poetry/General

Old Gods for New
Mike Algera

At a sidewalk sale
you will meet a dealer
he will tell you
he has monuments of old gods
for sale, "Pick a God,
and worship however you please."   ~ Excerpt from Old Gods for New

Old Gods for New reflects upon personal triumphs and demons, love and longing, the past and never-was; musings that spark both the artistry of playful banter as well as lyrical madness. Writing that is quirky yet daring, combining scratch words into something new.

$19.99
138 Pages
6" x 9"
ISBN-13: 978-0988075078
BISAC: Poetry/ General

Little Human Accidents:
Damon Ferrell Marbut

Damon Ferrell Marbut devastates the notion of apology in poetry with a tender recklessness in *Little Human Accidents*, poems that examine a personal evolution of sexuality and identity while treating the unavoidable step towards adulthood like a punching bag, especially in his free flowing self reflexive poems like *Mornings Like This* and *So What*.

$19.99
150 pages
6" x 9"
ISBN 13: 978-0988075092
BISAC: Poetry/ General

www.barebackpress.com

www.ingramcontent.com/pod-product-compliance
Lightning Source LLC
Chambersburg PA
CBHW070837030726
47504CB00005B/1126